# FIRE BOUND

# FIRE BOUND

## DRAGON OF SHADOW AND AIR BOOK TEN

JESS MOUNTIFIELD

DISRUPTIVE IMAGINATION

THE FIRE BOUND TEAM

**Thanks to our JIT Team:**

Diane L. Smith
Dave Hicks
Dorothy Lloyd
Deb Mader
Jeff Goode

*If We've missed anyone, please let us know!*

**Editor**
SkyHunter Editing Team

LMBPN Publishing supports the right to free expression and the value of copyright. The purpose of copyright is to encourage writers and artists to produce the creative works that enrich our culture.

The distribution of this book without permission is a theft of the author's intellectual property. If you would like permission to use material from the book (other than for review purposes), please contact support@lmbpn.com. Thank you for your support of the author's rights.

LMBPN Publishing
PMB 196, 2540 South Maryland Pkwy
Las Vegas, NV 89109

Version 1.00 November 2021
eBook ISBN: 978-1-68500-524-5
Print ISBN: 978-1-68500-525-2

*Dedication:*

*To those with faith in something bigger than themselves. It takes courage to hold on in the dark.*

# CHAPTER ONE

The tears stung my eyes as I listened to Minsheng. He was the only one who could give the eulogy for Ascan since he and Jinto had trained the young elf. While listening, I couldn't help but picture the relief on Ascan's face the first moment I'd met him.

It had been a rescue mission. Or so I'd thought. The organization had asked me to go to the aid of a Shishou and his ward and any other mythicals with them. I'd gone gladly, but all of them had been cult members who had infiltrated the organization. As Chris had. Of course, that didn't mean Ascan deserved to die.

The elf had switched his allegiance to the organization and the cause we fought, and Simon had killed him for it. Whenever I thought about it, my fists clenched, as they did now. I'd almost killed Simon for it.

No sooner had I thought that than I forced myself to relax again. It was my anger that had made everything worse. I'd been so intent on making Simon pay for Ascan's death I'd put myself right in harm's way. Zephyr had needed to break the pillars around the Mexican portal to save me.

As I relaxed, I looked down at my hand. I had grabbed a white-hot fragment of a rune-covered tablet to keep myself alive, and it had burned my hand. I was sure of it. The pain was in my memory. But there was only a faint mark on the palm of my hand when there should have been a burn. I would have told everyone if I wasn't wrapped up in guilt and wishing for punishment for what I had done.

On top of my guilt, Zephyr was plagued with it. Neither of us needed to say anything. Our bond meant that we, Sen, and Roth could feel it. It was coming off Zephyr and me in waves whenever we opened to each other. None of us were getting very close or letting the others in because of it. It wasn't fair or kind.

We stood in a ring around everyone else, as far back as we could get from the funeral before us, and still be polite. Zephyr was opposite me, his eyes downcast. He'd been brooding in his dragon form since it had happened. Sen stood on Minsheng's shoulders. Her mushroom top drooped, and her arms hung limply by her sides. Roth stood on the other side, Daisy and Emily leaning against the magnificent water pegasus, a wing tucked behind each of them.

I wanted to go to them, but I didn't feel as if I deserved them. Not anymore. I had mucked up so many times. They deserved a better mythical.

They slowly lowered Ascan's wicker coffin into the

ground. The earth elves grew the living structure around him. It was beautiful. They continued to grow it as they lowered him to the right depth.

When he was in place with the sapling of a tree above him, I stepped forward with earth elves. We moved the earth, slowly buried him, and closed the hole. It was the least I could do for someone I should have kept from harm.

Once that was done, Sierrathen said words I barely registered, acknowledging that lives came to an end but that life grew from what came before.

More tears threatened to fall. I tried to push them back, but my body disobeyed me. Even when they had stopped, I didn't move, trapped, staring at the small tree that represented the smiles and laughter, the dreams and passion that had been snuffed out.

"I don't know if saying it again will help, but none of this was your fault. None of it. Not even the portal being open now. You have always done your best at every turn against phenomenal odds. You can do no more."

Minsheng's words made the tears flow faster. He wrapped his arms around me and hugged me. I felt more hands reach out and rest on my shoulders and back and then Daisy hugged me as well. Sen was buried up against the side of my neck.

Zephyr and Roth also came closer, the large dragon the most hesitant. I calmed and looked sideways to meet Zephyr's gaze.

*It's not your fault either,* I said to him.

*I broke those pillars.*

"We'd have all broken those pillars to save Aella if we

could have done," Minsheng said, seeing the look passing between us and guessing what was being said so correctly it was almost scary.

"But it was still me who did it," Zephyr replied, his deep rumble so sorrowful I wanted to cry all over again.

"Yes. And to some degree, that burden can't be taken from your shoulders. But as much as we all are equal, in some ways we also aren't. You saved the only elf with enough power to lead us against the forces on the other side of that portal. And you saved yourself. You think you've doomed us all. We think you've given us the opportunity to fight another day and save us all."

Zephyr blinked as I sent a rush of warmth to him. It was true even if Zephyr didn't entirely feel it. I loved him still and he'd acted to save me. It was far more my fault than it was his.

"It's not your fault either, Aella," Zephyr said, fixing his attention on me. "Simon and the others lured us all deeper. They wanted the portals open and they did everything they could to make it happen. Simon is at fault for putting you in danger. And everyone who helped him."

"Speaking of Simon," Erlan said, "I have some news. But you're not going to like it and I don't think you will want to hear it here."

I lifted my eyebrows as Minsheng let me go, and Sen transferred to my shoulder. I wiped the last of the tears away, feeling calmer than I had in days.

"We'll be waiting for you at the remembrance meal. They'll understand that this is important. Go find somewhere quiet. If you need us to give you time and space, let us know," Minsheng said before he gave me another squeeze on the shoulder.

I nodded. Not sure that I liked the idea of missing the remembrance meal but seeing the look on Erlan's face made my mind up. I had a feeling this was going to be bad news, and given how Simon had reacted to Ascan betraying him, I had a feeling I was about to find out that my parents and Zephyr's mother were dead.

Reaching for the dragon, I placed a hand on his large shoulder, and we walked to a section of the Sanctuary with open space, near one of the small farm areas Gwaelon looked after.

Erlan went with us, a laptop tucked under one arm. It was clear he had been through the information he'd taken from the cult computers the last time we had been there. I was terrified of what he had discovered, but it was one of the reasons we'd gone there in the first place. I wanted answers, even if they hurt.

"Okay," I said as I sat down beside Zephyr. "Hit me with it."

The dragon's tail swished through the grasses until it was wrapped around me, and Sen snuggled into my neck some more. As Roth also knelt and then sat down beside me, I felt the warmth and love they expressed. If nothing else, I had my bonded mythicals.

"Your parents...well...you don't have any. Not exactly."

I lifted my eyebrows at Erlan's statement, not understanding a word of it. How could I not have parents?

"They made you in a lab, from sequenced DNA and incredibly clever combinations of dwarven, gnome, and elven magic. You were created from the DNA of great and powerful elves. From dragon and human DNA as well. They literally took a combination of strengths from every race they believed could contribute and melded you into the formidable warrior you are."

"But surely I'd have been implanted into someone? As an egg, or something."

"I think you were, but it was a quick pregnancy, and no mention is made of the mother or her name. I don't understand all the science, but essentially Simon used a team of mythicals to make you."

I exhaled, my vision blurring at the edges and my skin tingling all over. I wasn't normal. I wasn't even properly anything. I had no parents. How could I even exist? What was I? I wasn't an elf, or a human, not really.

*You're Aella-Faye Carter, Henera to the elves, bonded elf to a dragon, a dryad, and a pegasus. You brought mythicals into the light and defended them. You are the hope we all live for and the hope we now fight beside. You have a mind and use it to solve the world's problems. You have a body full of strength and magic and use it to protect those weaker. You have a heart and you love all those around you. You are everything you need to be and so much more.*

Zephyr's words echoed in my head as his tail squeezed me tighter. I felt as if I was going to be sick, but Sen and Roth leaned in and repeated the words, echoing them together.

By the time they were done, I was crying again, but I also felt stronger. Simon had made me in a lab, but he didn't define what I became. He had given me the building blocks of my life, but I was going to decide what I did with them.

"Thank you," I said to Erlan as I got up again. It wasn't his fault that he'd had to give me this news, and I wanted to reassure him. "Can you make sure I have a copy of everything? I think I'm going to want to look through it all and see if I can understand more."

"Of course. I already made a copy." Erlan held out a data stick and scrambled to his feet.

I took it and tucked it into my bag, grateful I had people like Erlan in my life. He gave me a nod and then headed away, going in the direction of the remembrance meal. Not sure what to do, I leaned toward Zephyr and put my hand on his smooth, warm scales.

Again I thought about the words my bonded mythicals had spoken over me. I didn't know how much of it I believed for sure, but I knew that their belief in me meant more than I could say. I wasn't alone. We'd face whatever was coming together, and I'd do my best not to let them down.

*I'm sorry*, I said to them. *I let guilt stop me from moving forward with you all. And this time is scary for everyone.*

I felt the warmth rush in from them. None of us needed to say anything else. We were in this together. Turning to look into Zephyr's eyes, I made sure he also felt better. We might have been responsible for opening the portals to some degree, but Minsheng had been right. Zephyr wouldn't have been the only one to have broken those pillars to save someone. I'd have done it for any one of the elves and mythicals in my world. All of us would have done it. It was what made us an effective fighting force. We would do whatever we could to keep each other alive.

It was what was going to keep us alive and fighting, whatever came through it.

With this thought, the four of us finally made our way to the meal. Ascan deserved our respect. He'd chosen to do what he thought was right rather than what others had tried to pressure him into. His memory was one I wanted to honor. I couldn't do that if I didn't show up because I was wallowing in self-pity.

Despite my resolve to do what was right, the nagging doubts wouldn't go away. What if we couldn't defeat what was coming through that portal? What if I wasn't the Henera? What if I was just a strange experiment gone wrong?

It seemed there was only one way to find out.

Of course, everyone still hoped that nothing would come through the portal. That the elves in the mountain would seal it the second they realized something was on the other side they didn't want to tangle with. Just as I had. Hopefully, it wouldn't be too late. Right now, I had no way of knowing. I only knew for sure that I wasn't welcome in that mountain.

As soon as I arrived at the meal, heads turned my way, many familiar faces there, including most of the council and the four elven masters. Minsheng quickly got up and came to me. I focused on him as I felt all eyes on me. I knew many of them were simply concerned for me, but it was hard to be comfortable under the scrutiny of so many gazes.

Walking toward Minsheng, I did my best to ignore it. Sen bounded from my shoulder and onto a nearby table before hopping onto the back of a foxlike creature I thought I recognized. It was sitting on the table near Seth, and he was laughing and joking with an ease I hadn't seen before.

Minsheng caught my gaze and leaned closer.

"He's bonded with it. They had the ceremony the day before we arrived back."

I grinned, knowing this was one of the things Seth had been salty about when we'd first met. Not every elf met the creature they were compatible with, and until recently, it hadn't been safe enough for most to go on a pilgrimage to find their bonded mythical either. I was happy for him.

As I caught his eye, I gave him a small smile and a nod, my gaze flicking to the creature long enough that he'd know why I was gesturing. It made the grin wider on his face, and he nodded back.

By the time he looked away and Sen came running back to me, I was no longer the center of everyone's attention. Feeling as if I could relax, I let Minsheng lead me and my mythicals to a seat, and we tucked into the food laid out for everyone. Around me, people were swapping stories that amused them or made them feel good things.

Most of the stories involved Ascan but some of them didn't, sparked by similar tales. It was truly wonderful to be surrounded by something so hopeful and uplifting. As I listened, I finally told a story of my own. How Ascan had stood beside me in training and shown his skill and bravery. How it had made me feel.

By the time the meal was over and elves were drifting back to their duties, I felt lighter, some of the grief having come out with the words and stories. If nothing else, Ascan had impacted many lives in lots of different ways, and to remember that had benefited us all.

Now it was time to get back to work, however. That meant seeing the Sanctuary council and working out what we were going to do. I also wanted to talk to the elven masters about my heritage and birthing process. I needed them to know what I was.

# CHAPTER TWO

It seemed I wasn't the only one who had thought about talking with the masters or the council. As I walked away from the meal tent, I saw the councilors and the masters gathered in the shade, drinks between them, and space for me and my mythicals. I also noticed that centaurs lingered nearby, keeping other elves and mythicals away for now.

I went to them, feeling the attention on me once more.

"Thank you for all you do, Aella," Sierrathen said as she stood.

Everyone else did as well, and then as one, they bowed. I stopped in my tracks, stunned and unsure what was being implied by the gesture.

Vestan smiled at the look on my face and held out his arm to usher me closer, his other hand motioning toward a seat near him.

"Come and sit. Erlan implied that you had received more difficult news, and I know you have suffered grief and loss. Not to mention the harm and danger you have faced. Sit and let us talk as friends."

I nodded, a lump in my throat preventing me from speaking at first. As my mythicals also got comfortable, Zephyr close enough I could have his tail flick around me and over my lap again, I calmed down.

Before any of the council could speak, I found myself confessing the truth of my life. What I knew about how I'd been created. There was silence until I'd finished speaking. Ruehnar got up and came closer. I tried not to look too surprised as he bowed again.

"Whatever brought you to us, I know one thing about you. You are the Henera. You have the DNA of the greats in you, no matter how that happened. And you are uniting us all. We will face whatever comes through those portals together. I know everyone sitting here feels exactly the same."

I looked around at the others as the water master sat back down again. There were smiles and nods, and Sierra then reached out and touched my hand.

"I can't imagine how lost this news must make you feel. Your journey has not been an easy one, and I'm ashamed to think about our early reception of you and how suspicious we were. I want you to know this place is as much your home as you want it to be. We are as much your family as you want us to be. I can't offer you parents or anything to fill that exact hole, but I can offer you acceptance and love."

"Hear, hear," Vestan added, and then it echoed around them.

Once more, I couldn't speak. Sen got up and danced, bouncing between the seated people until everyone was laughing.

It was exactly what I needed.

As Sen came back to rest on my lap, the atmosphere grew more serious, however. There were several matters to be addressed, but I expected the portal to be our focus. It was open.

"We have known that danger lies on the other side of these portals," Vestan said. "And we have known that the sect of elves who wish them open believe the danger is long gone or easily dealt with by yourself. But, please, tell us what you know and understand about these matters. You have a greater experience than many who now live. You've mentioned your belief that the evil still lingers. What can we expect?"

I sighed, wishing I could give them better and happier news, but I couldn't. I began by telling them of my experience connecting with something on the other side of the portal. It wasn't a happy tale, and I could see the faces around me growing serious. I also spoke of the way it had seemed easily defeated. While the way it had explored and probed at my bonds had hurt, I had easily shrugged it off once I understood its power and knew not to fight it head-on.

There was active relief at my words, although I noticed none of them offered an explanation for how this evil was trying to connect and what it had to do with the bonds I had with my mythicals. Finally, I retold the tale of how I had been led to the moment I had been knocked from the sky right into the forcefield of the pillars. How with so little power left, Zephyr had opted to break the pillars rather than let me die.

The last part of my story they had heard twice, but it was clear they wished to hear it again.

"I think it is right that we tell our people what has happened with the portals," Sierrathen said a moment later. "And we prepare to face whatever comes through."

"I agree. The more who understand the danger we are facing and begin preparing, the better," I replied, thinking about how few of the Sanctuary elves were currently capable of holding their own in organized battle. They would need to train, and the elven masters would need to be responsible for that part of things.

"Your heritage, however..." Vestan paused, and he looked almost apologetic.

I swallowed, waiting for him to continue, almost expecting him to declare me unfit to be called Henera anymore no matter how kind they had been to me.

"I think it's best that remains the secret it has been so far. While we still believe you to be Henera and nothing will change that, I worry that it might cause some to lose hope. And we need hope. It will keep everyone pushing harder, learning more, and preparing as much as possible."

Exhaling, relieved that it wasn't anything but a desire to be cautious, I quickly gave my assent to the comment. That I had been manufactured instead of here due to natural means wasn't something I wanted everyone to know, even if I had told the council without reservation.

"Then we must decide how we are going to prepare and gather the information we need," I said in reply. "War is coming, and we need to be as ready as we can be."

Before anyone could respond, there was a commotion by one of the centaurs, another coming running up, hooves thundering. Everyone's attention was turned that way as the two centaurs conversed, and then the newcomer was admitted. They ran to Ronan's side as if to report to him, but the council centaur motioned for the messenger to speak.

"Elves from Amcika have appeared. They have requested asylum, but they also requested to see the Henera and claim to have something that they believe belongs to her."

Shocked again, I didn't move. Was the day going to continue bringing me surprises, or would I get some relief at some point? I wasn't sure how I could keep enduring it, but I got the feeling this was going to be my life until the portals and the threat behind them were dealt with.

"Then I should see them and see what they bring with them. If others would wish to join me, they are welcome," I said as I got to my feet.

It was strange to lead a procession of mythicals, the council, and the greats, flanked by a centaur guard force as we made our way after the messenger to the area of the Sanctuary where the cult members had crossed.

Although I was tired, I was also curious. What could they want with the Sanctuary and me? And what gift could they have for me? There was only one way to find out, and I was relieved when the group came into view. Four elves sat on the ground surrounded by mythicals brandishing weapons, Seth among them and everyone looking tense.

I reached out a hand and motioned for the guards to lower weapons.

"There's no harm these four can do that the council and I couldn't prevent. Please, everyone, relax and tell me what this is about."

As I finished speaking, I looked at the nearest of the

Amcika elves, recognizing his face as one of the ones I'd fought in the past. He slowly got to his feet, holding his hands out to make it clear he was trying to be peaceful, and then looked at me.

"We need your help, Henera. I know we don't necessarily deserve it, and you may not care for our lives, but I fear Cherisse and Simon have gone too far. The portal doesn't hold the promise we hoped for."

I had to fight back the urge to make a quip about having told them and instead nodded, hoping he was here to do more than confirm my suspicions and ask me to do something I wasn't necessarily capable of.

"Will you return to the mountain with us and help us close the portal?" the elf asked.

"Cherisse wants to see it closed?" I asked, my surprise clear in my voice. "Already? What happened?"

"Cherisse doesn't want to see it closed. At least, not yet. She still believes there are plenty of elves on the other side who need our aid and would be better off here on earth. But we think the risk is too great. Three times the portal has opened and brought elves here, and three times they have attacked us, their faces and bodies like those of mindless drones sent to perform the task of their maker. The world on the other side of the portals is not the friendly place we hoped it would be."

I frowned. That wasn't something I had hoped to hear. Not only did Cherisse not want me there, but it wasn't going well and three attacks in such a short space of time was worse than any of us had feared. But I wasn't going somewhere I wasn't invited.

"Did you successfully rebuff each attack?" I asked.

"We did. But each one was stronger than the last. And each time, many of the...elves returned through the portal. As if they were reporting back. We fear they are trying to learn what they are up against to mount a far larger attack."

"That is possible," I replied. "But unless I am welcomed into the mountain by Cherisse and Simon, I am not sure there is much I can do about it. I understand your concern and feel it too, but it isn't my duty to stop others from suffering the consequences of their own actions. Amcika has gotten exactly what they wished for."

The moment I finished speaking, there was silence, and I found myself wondering if I had been too unkind and unempathetic, but the elf nodded.

"I feared you would react so. It is understandable, and you are right. And I also understand that unless Cherisse and Simon see the need to have your aid that there might not be much you can do. But I had hoped you'd be willing to try to persuade them. If that is not the case, there is still one reason we came to find you." With this, the elf reached into a small bag he carried and pulled out a wrapped parcel.

After a brief pause, he stepped closer and held it out to me. I raised an eyebrow as I took the package and unwrapped it, hearing the clank of metal from inside. A moment later I gasped, holding the fire belt of the great elven master.

"Do you know what this is?" I asked as I looked at the cult members.

"I suspected. It was passed to a friend of mine in the mountain when his father died. He was pretty sure it was some great artifact and was told to give it to someone worthy. But he told several of us about it. When Sarai looked into the books in the library on artifacts of power, it mentioned four from the greats and how only a descendant could wield them."

I looked at the girl he motioned to and nodded. This looked as if it matched the artifact Orthelo had asked me to find. But could I truly wield it? I hadn't yet been able to use the fire element. And so far, I'd not used an artifact for an element I didn't control.

*Try to put it on. If it isn't something you're ready for, it won't work*, Zephyr said.

I wasn't sure it was a good idea to do so in front of the cult elves, but I needed to know, and I didn't want to waste time. Once again, I looked at the small mark on my hand and wondered if it was a sign that I was ready for the belt. Zephyr was right. There was only one way to find out.

Taking a deep breath and trying not to look too nervous, I unclasped it and reached it around my waist. As the bracers, ring, and necklace had done, it sensed that it was about my waist and gently tightened until it fit snugly, the clasp closing with a click. My senses came alive in a whole new way. I could feel the strange consuming hunger of a nearby fire and the way the heat in my body felt as it was created and then used.

I blinked, surprised at the sudden clarity and how it amplified sensations within me that I had begun to feel. I was sure now that I had absorbed the heat from the rock I'd grabbed, spreading it through my body and dispersing it into the ground. That fire was something I had begun controlling, but so subtly it had gone unnoticed.

Just as each of the other three elements had felt very

different to control and connect with, this one was different again. Where the air felt like it flowed around and over, a light sensation that filled the mind, the plants and earth felt like a steady, stable presence that grew and moved beside, the water something that you became part of, the fire was something that raged and consumed, first in one form and then another.

The fire element felt easily the most chaotic and unpredictable, the fiercest. If Seth's body felt as if it was raging with potential anywhere near the way mine did, it made it clear that Seth gained some of his hot-headed nature from his skill with the element. My ability to control the fire element also partially explained how I had struggled to keep calm recently. I had an inferno inside me. And it did not want to be controlled.

"You truly are Henera," Sierrathen said, reminding me that the council and the elven masters were looking on. I turned to them, feeling my cheeks flush. I hadn't checked with the fire master that he was happy for me to have the belt, nor that Orthelo didn't feel upset that I hadn't found the belt, but it had been brought to me anyway.

My fears were washed away, however, as the nearby elves got down on one knee. I gaped, not sure what to do or say. This wasn't what I'd expected. I quickly encouraged them to their feet, not wanting to feel as if I was the subject of adoration I didn't deserve.

"I'm still me," I said, not sure how else to convey how awkward I felt. "I've gotten funky superpowers and I train hard, but I'm still Aella."

I saw Gwaelon's mouth twitch into a smile, but no one else disagreed or reacted other than to congratulate me.

I was about to get the others to focus on the cult members again and what they were going to do or where they were going to go when I heard a strange bird-like trill. At the same time, I was aware of a presence. An extremely hot presence. And it was flying toward me faster than I'd have thought anything could fly.

Looking toward it, I noticed Orthelo and Bialan were doing the same. What could they sense that I could as well?

A moment later, I spotted the beautiful plumage of the phoenix Orthelo had been caring for. It came toward me like a firebolt streaking through the sky. My eyes went wide, my heart barely beating as what this could mean filled my head.

Before I could form a coherent thought, the bird flew close, slowed, and then circled my head. There was a flash of bright light, and everyone gasped. My head was filled with the thoughts and feelings of the strange young bird.

*Hello*, I thought gently, still in shock. I'd stood in the same room with the bird before and not bonded with it. Had putting on the belt and boosting my fire element changed my power so much that a bond was possible when it hadn't been before?

I had no idea, but from the wide-eyed stares I was getting, especially from Bialan and Orthelo, I wasn't the only one surprised I'd bonded with a phoenix.

CHAPTER THREE

Several minutes had passed since the firebird had flown across the Sanctuary to be with me. He sat on my shoulder as if it was a familiar spot. Sen stood on the other, and Zephyr and Roth had come closer.

Although everyone had wanted to ask questions, Bialan and Orthelo had cleverly maneuvered me and my mythicals off to one side out of concern for the fragile bird. It had been under Orthelo's care for several years. I had seen him nurse it into the beautiful bird it was now.

*Do you have a name?* I asked, still not sure the creature understood me. His thoughts were a jumble of words and images, moving so fast I had trouble keeping up.

*Nuri*, the bird eventually replied. I blinked; his voice was deeper than I'd expected. It was a strange, melodic sound, and he calmed as he said it.

*Aella*, I replied, before introducing the other mythicals I was bonded with, doing the introductions while I wrapped my head around what was happening. I was still not sure I believed it. Of all the majestic creatures to have bonded with, I had four of the most amazing, and it was a blessing I didn't deserve.

I listened as Zephyr, Sen, and Roth made Nuri feel welcome. It relieved me. I was aware of the others staring at us. Orthelo was beaming with pride, and Bialan's eyes had lit up.

As soon as I thought Nuri was happy and content, I gave the council and elven masters my attention again.

"I think you've probably worked out that Nuri and I bonded."

"Nuri?" Orthelo asked. "That's the perfect name."

"You didn't name him?" I blinked.

"No. Most mythicals like to choose their name or receive one from their parents. I wait until they tell me. But a phoenix never speaks unless they bond with an elf and the elf teaches them."

Looking at Nuri, I felt a flush of pride. I might not deserve to be bonded with another mythical, but I was very grateful to be. I was still overwhelmed by the new ability and awareness of it and the new mind connected to mine.

"Why don't I talk Aella through some uses of the fire? Then, if all is well, we can inform the Sanctuary of the bonding ceremony that we all, no doubt, wish to see," Bialan said as he stepped forward.

I nodded, grateful that he was suggesting everyone give me some space. I needed it. This was an unexpected change in my life. I'd have thought I would need to get to grips with the element before I could bond with another mythical. Instead, one was on my shoulder, and a huge new power had unlocked inside me.

Bialan led me to a small clearing away from everyone,

especially the cult elves who were still being guarded. Zephyr and Roth followed, with Sen and Nuri on my shoulders. I could feel the lightness of the firebird and marveled that he was almost as light as Sen despite being so much larger.

I could also feel radiance coming off him, warmth and light despite him being nothing but brightly colored feathers. It made me wonder how true the myths about the phoenix were. Could they become literal balls of flame?

"I believe so," Bialan replied when I asked.

*Yes. I think I remember the great fire elf having a phoenix as his bonded creature,* Zephyr added.

*Zaos,* Nuri joined in. *Zaos was mine.*

*You bonded with Zaos?* I asked, my jaw falling open.

*Zaos my elf. We bond. Long time ago. Many fire lives since then.*

*You've lived that long?*

*Nuri reborn again and again. World changed many times.*

*It sounds like it would have. I'm honored I could bond with you.*

*Nuri feel Zaos in you. And much else. Nuri honored.*

I reached up a hand and gently stroked his feathers, feeling the warmth of his body and hoping that he wouldn't become a fireball while sitting on my shoulder.

"Right. Shall we go over basics so you don't set light to things you don't want to, or let it get out of control?" Bialan asked a moment later.

I gave him my consent, curious about the element I'd gained as well as the new bond. I was aware that I also had a new dynamic to get used to again. Thankfully my mythicals focused as well. I set some fires and snuffed them out, then Zephyr took human form beside me.

This was rare for him, but there was little point to him hiding it and he wanted to practice as well. Nuri flew off my shoulder and became a flaming ball of light that darted around our heads. Roth sucked up water from a nearby barrel. Instead of shooting it out as water, something happened inside of him.

I watched as he let off an orange glow, shimmering the way sunset did on the water, then jetted out a combination of hot steam and water.

Bialan clapped his hands.

"Yes, I had hoped that you would be able to combine the elements. It is remarkable and wonderful. I can see why being an elf with four elements makes you better than four elves with the same strength at each. You can combine them, and your mythicals can fight in ways others can't. You're more than the sum of your parts. And able to communicate so much more swiftly and intuitively."

"But the elf... The evil one on the other side of the portal. He can control all the elements as well if I understand correctly," I said.

"I believe so. But I cannot say for sure. I only know what has been said in the past about him. I didn't live to see his reign. I confess I hoped I would never live to see him return."

"He hasn't yet. We'll stop it before it starts if we can," I said, realizing I believed my words.

Bialan looked at me.

"If anyone else had said that to me, I would have called it arrogance and naïveté, but there's something about you and what you're capable of. And there's something about everything you've achieved. You make me believe it's possible to win this."

"I can't promise it will be easy. Or that everyone will survive," I added, thinking about Ascan and Lorcan. It was a small miracle that we'd lost only two mythicals whom I knew so far.

"I wouldn't ask you to. But I have hope that for whoever remains, the world will be a brighter place. And it will have been down to the changes you are fighting for. And the evil you're fighting against."

I sighed, hoping the fire master was right. I wanted to see the world and the elves, mythicals, humans, dwarves, and gnomes who lived here safe once more. There had to be a way to get everyone through this.

There was going to be a bonding ceremony for us. This was no small task. We'd done two before, but each time it felt as if I needed to do more and show our teamwork and how it could make us more formidable.

This bonding ceremony was about hope. Hope when everyone was finding out that the evil they feared could come through a portal at any moment.

As soon as Bialan was happy that I had enough control over the fire and I wasn't so overwhelmed, he called to the other masters who were nearby to work on a ceremony performance.

While we had been planning, several elves had checked in on us, and the cult elves had been escorted somewhere else. I got the impression it wasn't the last I'd seen of them. If nothing else, I needed to thank them for bringing me the belt.

By the time we had a plan for the ceremony and were sure we could pull off our respective elements, I was eager to get it done. I could tell news had spread among the Sanctuary that it was going to be happening. We joined the mythicals making their way to the cave where the ceremonies were held.

I noticed the cave entrance was wider than it used to be. As Zephyr went inside, back in dragon form, I could tell it was taller as well. When we reached the main meeting hall, I gaped. It was bigger again, and it made me wonder what had happened to it.

Sierrathen saw me looking around and came to my side.

"We had the earth elves make a bigger space. Took them a lot less time than I thought it would. The council agreed that the entire city was going to want to see you and the new bond. It's been a long time since an elf has bonded with a phoenix. And you are Henera," she explained quietly.

I gulped. This was a lot of pressure. The entire city was watching us, and we hadn't rehearsed.

*Nuri isn't new to a bond and the rest of us have fought beside you many times. This will be like a walk in the park,* Zephyr said as his head lowered to bump gently into me.

*We've never walked in a park.*

*No, but we've fought parkfuls of enemies. That counts, right?*

I chuckled, not sure how to reply to that. It amused and distracted me enough that it did the job. Sierrathen expertly guided us to the center of the cave and began getting us into position.

We formed a pentagon, with the crowds radiating out from that.

Despite the widened area, I noticed that the space where we would perform the bonding ceremony was still smaller than it had been the first time. We were given the now-familiar stones, placed on the ground behind us. We were supposed to turn and pick them up or touch them and they'd light up, but I was hoping we could be more spectacular than that.

Grinning, Sierrathen took her place and looked around. Silence rippled outward, the expectation that we were about to begin enough to silence the majority of the cavern.

I took a deep breath to steady myself and then reached out to the elements around us. Feeling four of them respond was almost overwhelming at first. The air and earth were natural and the water was getting that way, so it was just the fire and warmth in the room that took me by surprise.

There was a strangeness to it as well. I could feel the heat in everybody in the room, but I could also feel the light in the sun as it was projected around the cavern by the carefully placed mirrors and crystals. I could feel the torchlight and large open fires scattered around to increase the light and warmth. It was phenomenal.

"Over the last few years, we have witnessed the growth of an elf into a formidable warrior. Alongside her are several mythicals who have bonded to her and proved their worth and integrity as well. Today our Henera has gained her final element and her final bond and will demonstrate her knowledge, skill, and worthiness with the four elements and mythicals she has been bestowed with." Sierrathen paused as the cavern cheered.

It was deafening, and I wanted to run and hide. This was huge, and I didn't know if I could handle being the center of this much attention. As Zephyr sent waves of calm my way, however, I focused on the mythicals with me. They had bonded with me and trusted me. I needed to live up to that trust if nothing else.

"Only once in our history has such a display of power and control been shown, and it was forced in a way this wasn't," Sierrathen continued. "Today, you will witness the beauty of nature finding its balance. Of mythicals in harmony."

This was our cue to turn back to our stones, pick them up, and then see them light up, but we'd opted to do something different. Instead of picking them up, we simply touched them and turned our backs on them again. As I did so I exhaled, terrified that one of them wouldn't light up even though they had in the past. I could feel Nuri in my head and stomach the way I did the others. There was no reason for me to doubt my bonds. But I was also distracted by Sierrathen's words.

This had happened before. Was she talking of the evil elf everyone was so scared of? Was that why I could feel him searching along the bonds I had whenever we'd connected through the portal? Had he found a way to force a bond between him and other mythicals?

*It would seem like it,* Zephyr replied. *And my ancestors believed he had corrupted something. But we cannot focus on this now. You need to concentrate on the fire and make sure no one gets hurt.*

Zephyr's words reminded me of what we were doing. There was cheering and clapping. I turned to see the mythicals and the brightly lit stones near us. In the past, they had been the same color, but I noticed that this time, each was different. The one in front of Zephyr was a pale brown, green for Sen, blue for Roth, red for Nuri, and in front of me, it was glowing a brilliant white.

There were gasps, and Sierrathen was looking at them with wide eyes. I had a feeling that this wasn't normal either.

As we stood there, the chatter grew. Before too much could be made of the stones, I reached for the fire in the nearest brazier and pulled it toward me in an arc across the top of the crowds.

There was silence again. Before the fire could touch me Roth leaped up, hitting it with water and putting it out. Before he'd finished doing so, I'd grabbed another, and Nuri dealt with this one as Roth sucked in more water and made a pool for Sen to leap into. Nuri blocked the fire with his body, turning into a fireball and then flying overhead with it.

As I grabbed a third, Sen formed ice bolts and pelted it, the fire and ice coming together in a crackling, fizzing cacophony until there was nothing left but a watery mess. The fourth streak of fire I took control of went Zephyr's way. He didn't react at first, but then he opened his mouth and simply swallowed the whole thing.

A moment later, he burped it back out again, controlled and right in front of him.

I grinned as Nuri then flew through that as well, growing brighter.

As soon as they were back in the position I calmed and did the same thing to them again but at the same time. Once more, they dealt with the fire and showed that it couldn't harm them.

We followed the display by taking to the air as I reached out for the water as well. While we flew, Sen with help, there were more gasps of awe and wonder. I still needed to incorporate water before I used the ground to help us land. I made the stream that still flowed through the roof from my last visit emit fog and I pulled it toward us.

Zephyr ate it, Roth absorbed it, and Sen and Nuri burst right through it, their bodies seemingly unaffected. I'd expected Nuri to struggle, but steam merely rose from him on the other side, giving him a vapor trail.

After flying around each other, weaving, dipping, and displaying how well we could fly and not hit each other or slow each other down, I reached for the earth.

I brought the ground up to meet us as Zephyr transformed into a human in mid-air and landed. As he landed, he grew a plant that caught Sen. Nuri alighted in the branches of it. Roth and I landed on either side of him a moment later.

We were in a line, each of us brandishing an element and looking fierce. I panted, having lost myself in the moment but now aware of the entire crowd.

This time the cheers were deafening, and I winced as someone clapped me on the back. Sierrathen lifted her hands, tears in her eyes.

The bonding ceremony was officially over, and I had a feeling we were considered the greatest mythicals ever to live. It was a lot to take in.

# CHAPTER FOUR

I was stuffed, and I thought I might burst. I excused myself from the feast. It was strange to think we'd buried Ascan only hours earlier. The mood had changed from sorrow to celebration, but our bonding was a huge thing for many in the Sanctuary.

I had more questions, however, and I had a lot more responsibility. While I'd had fewer than four elements, I had convinced myself that it wasn't a big deal to be Henera. Or that I might not be the Henera in the prophecy. With four elements and bonds and the portals now being open, it was beginning to feel as if this whole prophecy thing had more weight to it.

There was no way I could ignore it any longer, and I wanted more information. I wanted to know what I was supposed to do, what I was up against, and what was going on in that mountain.

I went to find the cult elves in the Sanctuary first. It was the simplest piece of the puzzle. I needed to know what was happening in the here and now, find out what I might face, and why Cherisse wasn't asking for my help but they were.

The Sanctuary had taken them to a similar place as the last two cult elves. I found six of them together, deep in conversation.

As soon as they saw me and the four mythicals who trooped after me, Zephyr in dragon form, they sat up, the picnic they had been sharing forgotten. I would have asked if they'd seen the bonding ceremony or enjoyed the feast that happened afterward, but I got the feeling they hadn't been invited.

It bothered me even if they couldn't be trusted. They smiled and bowed toward me as the centaurs did.

"I'm glad the great belt of Zaos took to you, Henera," the elf who had given it to me said. "It makes it easier on our minds to know we did something helpful by bringing it to you."

"You have my gratitude," I replied, also bowing to show respect. It couldn't have been easy for them to get to the Sanctuary to give it to me.

"We know we don't have much right to ask for it, but we'd appreciate your support. We wish to return to the mountain and the portal. We feel we should be doing everything we can to stop the evil one from coming through and to close it again if we can. But we would appreciate your help."

"Because Cherisse doesn't feel the same?" I asked, wanting to be sure.

"No," the lead male elf said. "She still believes that there are elves on the other side who need our aid and will come to ours."

"There is a chance she is right," I said, thinking about the elf I had once connected with through the portal who had seemed friendly and ecstatic to find a kind elf on the other side. No matter how many times I'd been near the Texas portal since I'd not felt her again, however.

"I do not think it is worth the risk. Not to everyone here."

"How many think like you in the mountain?" I asked, agreeing with their sentiment.

There was an awkward silence as they looked between themselves.

"Only you four," I said for them.

Two of them nodded while the other pair looked down.

"I can't promise to help you," I said. If I wasn't wanted, there wasn't much I could do. "But I do promise to come and lend aid the second Cherisse asks for it personally."

I reached into my pocket and pulled out a burner cell phone that Minsheng had gotten me. It was being kept active by the organization in case I needed it. I hoped they'd understand as I handed it over.

"Take this with you. There's a number in it that will reach my Shishou. Use it if things change. And if I find myself coming your way anyway, I'll reach out and let you know."

They blinked, and I had a moment of worry that they wouldn't know how to work it, but they quickly checked it was working and the number stored in it, showing my fear was baseless.

"It's not what we hoped, but it's something we can accept," the male in charge said as he got to his feet.

"I have a lot of answers to find, and I'll do what I can to

help protect this planet, but if *he* hasn't come through and he's being held back for now, then my time is better spent gathering information and figuring out if we can rescue other people. I cannot be everywhere at once, and there is still much to understand."

This made them happier, but I could see they were weary and tired. It was all I could give them, however. I bowed to them once more. They went back to their picnic, and I walked away with Zephyr.

*For what it's worth, I think you chose correctly. We can't easily help somewhere we're not wanted*, he said.

*I hope you're right.*

We didn't get much farther, intending to head to the masters' training area to practice the new ability and train together as a group of five. Before we could, Minsheng came hurrying up.

"What is it?" I asked.

"The Texas portal. The President has asked for our advice and aid as swiftly as possible."

Before Minsheng had finished speaking, Zephyr had morphed into dragon form, and I was feeling for the air. If something was happening at another portal, then we were in big trouble.

"What do you know?" I asked as I hurried to get my away bag, grateful I'd find it packed and knowing Minsheng's wouldn't be far from it. We'd learned to live ready to leave at a moment's notice.

"Not much. They said there's no immediate danger of the portal opening as far as they can tell, but its behavior is erratic, and they want to make sure."

I frowned, not liking the sound of that. The strange

unclean feeling I'd been left with every time Kirdash had connected with me across the portal came flooding back. I didn't want to be anywhere near him or anything he controlled, but if I truly was the Henera everyone said I was, then I was going to have to fight him at some point.

As I grabbed my bag and slung it on my back, I made sure Nuri and the others were good to fly.

*I'll carry Minsheng if you can fly some of the way,* Zephyr said.

*I can carry Aella for a short while,* Roth offered. *My strength has grown with use and better care in the last few days.*

*Nuri fly always,* the firebird added.

*Sen ride,* she said with a grin.

I looked between them and nodded, grateful that if nothing else, I had them working with me. Within another couple of minutes, we were in the air, hurrying to Texas and whatever was wrong there.

Having made the journey so many times, it felt effortless. Even with flying well over half the distance and only taking a short break to let Roth carry me, I was feeling full of energy when I spotted the Texas site and we landed in front of it.

The soldiers looked suspicious when Nuri landed on my shoulder and preened.

"It's okay. He's with me," I said when the major quickly came out of the main building and his eyes went wide.

"Is that the mythical creature I think it is?" he asked.

I grinned and nodded.

"I have all four of my elements and all four bonds now," I replied, wondering how often I was going to have to explain it over the course of the next few days. There was a surprisingly large number of people in my life now.

"I wish I had time to ask you about it, but the portal has gone crazy again. It's blowing the readings like it does when you say that you've felt a presence on the other end." The major spoke while turning back to the main building and the portal, so he didn't see the shudder that tore through me.

Hearing that the evil was possibly lurking right on the other side of the portal was terrifying. I wasn't ready to face him, and I could only hope it wasn't Kirdash. Minsheng was also concerned. He reached into his pack for his instruments and then handed off the rest with my away pack to a couple of soldiers who rushed to aid us.

"To the portal then," I said. My stomach tightened into knots.

*We'll be careful,* Zephyr said. *And if need be, back off.*

*I wish I knew I could fight him.*

*We can. You're not alone, remember. We can fight his attempts to do anything with our bonds as well.*

It was a good point and one that made me relax.

*Nuri fought Kirdash before. Nuri teach.*

The phoenix's words echoed around my head as I looked at him in surprise. Of course Nuri would know about Kirdash and the fight that Zaos and the other great elves had been a part of.

I had so many questions, but it wasn't the time. Instead, we hurried toward the portal, eager to find out what was going on.

No sooner had I gotten halfway up the corridor than I could feel the strangeness to the air. I noticed many of the soldiers had fallen back, the offices and meeting rooms closest to the portal emptying of people. The general spotted me and came over.

"It's as if the pillar forcefield is expanding, but without the potency," the general explained.

I lifted my eyebrows, having no idea what could be causing the pillars to expand.

*It's not pillars. Kirdash does this*, Nuri said a moment later. *Pillars were the idea he gave Tuviel.*

"Get everyone back and out of it. It's not the pillars, but it's not good to remain in it either. I'll handle this as best I can."

The general took one glance at me and the determined look I was giving him and started barking orders. It helped that most of the people in the building had been instinctively doing the suggested activity, and within a minute, they were clear.

*Right, this could feel pretty rough*, I said to my mythicals, warning them and showering them with a wave of affection so they'd know we were in this together.

With that, I stepped forward and reached for the elements. I could feel the control over them and how something slimy was crawling along the surfaces.

I pushed it back, snapping the control of the elements out of his grip and into mine, allowing us to feel relief. The area ahead felt as if the dark elf was struggling to connect farther out. I didn't know how much I wanted to push him back.

*Consider it practice?* Zephyr asked.

I exhaled, not sure I wanted that kind of practice, but not sure there was an alternative idea I liked the sound of. I was going to have to push this guy back. If nothing else, the portal site needed to be secure, and that meant I needed to keep him at bay and make him realize there was one elf here powerful enough to stop him.

As I felt farther forward, making sure I had control of what I'd taken, I felt the dark elf's mind. Once more he latched onto me, connecting in a way that hurt but was strangely compelling. It sickened me, however. This wasn't something I wanted.

I fought, pushing him back as I'd learned to do on previous occasions. There was no way he was getting anywhere near my bonded mythicals. But the evil that lay on the other side of the portal seemed to be expecting me.

*Hello again, my dear,* a deep gravelly voice reverberated through my head. *You must be Henera.*

I winced as the grip on me grew, the words distracting me enough that I'd stopped fighting quite as hard. I pushed back not uttering a word but feeling Nuri leaning in closer to me, his mind sending calming thoughts that helped take away some of the pain.

Over the next few minutes, Nuri sent feelings and directions to me over the bond, seemingly unaffected by what was happening and guiding me to better fight the grip of the dark elf.

Slowly I pushed him back, concentrating on that one task as I kept hold of the elements around me, Nuri directing me into taking a sideways approach. As suddenly as his mind appeared and the attack began, it ended, the presence retreating.

I exhaled as my mind flew forward, almost following

him to the portal and back through. The area he'd been controlling went quiet, his mind gone from that as well.

Hurrying forward physically, I realized I had been oblivious to anyone else, so locked in battle that anything could have happened around me.

"What did you do?" Minsheng asked as I jogged toward the portal, my Shishou barely keeping up.

"I fought him until he either gave up or something happened on his end," I replied, deciding to be open about how little I knew.

"It was the dark one then?"

"It felt like it. He knew I was Henera."

"He spoke to you?"

"Yes," I replied, shuddering as I reached the edge of the normal forcefield and stopped.

I took in the area around the portal. The barriers, equipment, and anything else man-made that stood out about a yard or two was wrecked. It was a charred, smoking mess. I tried not to worry about it as I looked around and instead focused on the portal.

It was closed, and the pillars were functioning like normal. Given how Kirdash had managed to control the elements in the room, it made me wonder why he hadn't broken the pillars. Was that something he could do?

I pointed it out to Minsheng and felt the elements in the forcefield and around the pillars. Although my mind was very tired, I needed to know if anything was stopping him from breaking the pillars.

"All the destruction he's wrought is outside the pillars, and I don't detect anything that suggests his presence inside the forcefield. It feels like it normally does. It also appears to be the normal readings in the pillar zone."

Frowning, I checked the stone towers and the elements outside the forcefield. I could feel a marker where Kirdash had taken control of the elements and manipulated them, but everything in the pillars was unmarked. For some reason, Kirdash either couldn't or wouldn't break the pillars, but he could reach through the portals and break a lot of other things.

# CHAPTER FIVE

Sitting at the main meeting table, I shoveled food in, and Nuri pecked at the flesh of some fruit I'd cut up for him. I listened to Minsheng explain the data he had and what we thought it might mean to the President, the general, the major, and several other key personnel at the Texas portal site. It wasn't information anyone was happy about, but it was important for them to know.

I had a dull headache, and it reminded me that my brief encounter with Kirdash, the dark elf on the other side of the portal, had been incredibly taxing. Although I hadn't been at full strength when I had taken him on, I had been pushed hard, and Nuri proved my saving grace against him.

This had been an eye-opener for me. Something had made Kirdash feel through this portal. And he'd greeted me by title if not by name. Had he been trying to get my attention knowing he'd connected to me here before? The last time I had fought him, it had been at the Mexican portal deep in the mountain the cult lived in.

That portal was open, but I didn't know if he had attempted to go through it. If he hadn't, why not? Could the cult hold him back somehow? Was something else going on that I didn't understand?

There were so many questions buzzing around my head and no clear answers to any of them. Dwelling on them only made things worse, but I kept wanting to hope that I had missed something. Something that would help us strategize and plan a good way to end Kirdash and his plot. Whatever that was.

With Minsheng done and everyone filled in, there was nothing but silence. It was clear that the people in the room were struggling to process everything that they'd been told. It was a lot to take in, and I wasn't surprised. If I hadn't experienced so much of what was being talked about firsthand, I was pretty sure I'd be struggling as well.

"How are we going to defend against this dark elf if we can't stop him from reaching through the portal and attacking the protective forcefield?" the major asked.

"I don't think he can attack the forcefield directly," I said, bringing everyone's attention to me. "Given how much he was trying to get me and the cult to open them and let him in, I think that for some reason, he can't. But that doesn't mean he can't break things, hurt people, and cause chaos. I think he's angry and wants control."

"Sounds as if he's psychotic," the general replied.

I noticed the President's face became grimmer and found myself wondering what the country's leader was thinking. How much of a threat did he feel this dark elf was?

He looked up, and our eyes met as he stood.

"I think Aella is right. This dark elf wants that portal open, and that's with the Mexican one already so. If he could open it, he would have done so already. I want everyone here to be as safe as possible, however. I'd like to invite Minsheng to stay and help us find a way to monitor the portal and the activity. To get as much warning as we can that it's about to go haywire."

"That should be doable with a little help," Minsheng replied, giving the man a nod.

"Our elves are as needed as ever. With the exception of Aella, I would request that you all stay and continue to help us protect the area from the dark elf. I can't pretend to understand exactly how your powers work, nor how this dark elf tries to manipulate things, but I do know that we need you to help us if we're to keep everyone here safe. Would you consider staying and lending your aid?"

Seth nodded without hesitation on behalf of the elves on the base, disturbing the fire fox on his lap. Most of them were Sanctuary elves, and I had no doubt that they were willing, but I was also aware that some of them were elves from the warehouse.

I made a mental note to check the warehouse elves were okay and consult with Seth before I realized that the President had other plans for me. He'd said I was an exception, but he was already ushering most of the soldiers and elves out of the room and talking to the general.

*He probably wants us to go to Mexico too,* Zephyr said.

*Yay! That sounds like so much fun.*

*It would be if they had pizza.*

I laughed aloud, drawing the attention of the rest of the room. Zephyr always knew how to lighten the mood, and I could feel Sen chuckle while Roth smiled. Nuri looked confused, and I made a mental note to introduce the fire-bird to pizza as soon as possible. Assuming his digestion could handle it.

Once everyone but Minsheng, the general, and the President had left, the room was as empty as it was going to get. Thankfully Zephyr had space to breathe, though the room was not big enough for him in dragon form. He could have taken human form, of course, but it still required effort, and he preferred to be in dragon form around those who barely knew him.

I got up, wondering if I should leave as well, but every-one's attention returned to me again, and no one moved out of my path to the door.

"So, what are you going to ask me to do?" I asked before anyone could say anything.

"This other portal. Do you know if this dark elf will try to come through it?" the President asked, confirming Zephyr's statement.

"I have no idea, but he's sending something through it. The elves in the mountain are the only line of defense. They're a strong unit, though, and used to fighting other elves. As far as lines of defense go, they're a good one."

"That might be true, but it sounds as if you're the only one with direct experience against him, and the only two mythicals with direct memories are bonded to you," the President said.

I swallowed, knowing where this was going. I was being asked to go to the portal, if not to stay and actively defend it, to gather more information. And a part of me hated the idea of taking orders, even if it wasn't anything different to my wishes anyway. I was getting used to giving them and not answering to anyone.

*I don't think you've ever taken orders well,* Zephyr replied, the snark to his voice obvious.

Again I had to fight not to laugh. He was probably right, but either way, I was glad that after everything we'd been through in the last few years that my dragon still had his sass and sense of humor.

"You have a point," I said aloud, instead of the many other thoughts that had gone through my head. "But I'm sure I'm not welcome."

"I'm sure you're not. But they need you more than they realize, just like we did. And if there is one thing I know for sure in all this, it's that you and your mythicals are willing to do what's right, even if the world appears to disagree."

Opening my mouth, I considered objecting, but it was true. I *had* done what I intended, so why didn't I want to go to the mountain to help Cherisse and the other elves keep the portal safe and possibly close it up again? Why was I trying to stay out of this one when I wasn't willing to do the same before?

Before any of us could say any more, Minsheng's device on the table started beeping.

"Portal's active again," he said.

I rushed toward the door and the portal. This time everyone moved out of my way, and I led the four mythicals that were bonded to me into the hallway and through the canvas barrier that blocked the portal from the main building. I could feel the tension in the air as my skin itched with it.

I got as close as I dared and took control of as much of the air, earth, water, and fire around the forcefield as I could. It wasn't easy to hold such a large area, but it was necessary if I was going to make it clear to the dark elf on the other side that I wasn't messing around and I had the power to stop him if I chose.

I held the extra water I had in the air and waited. If the dark elf was on the other side of the portal and the one pushing through, I wanted to make sure I was in the way. But if it was something or someone else, then hopefully, I wasn't about to scare them off.

I continued to wait, feeling the pillars and forcefield pulse as if pushed out. Although I wasn't sure what was going on, I was aware that something was interrupting the usual spread and calm of the forcefield when everything within it was fine, but not sure what or how yet.

Concentrating, I reached forward with my mind. I could feel rather than see my mythicals move to the side as everyone else important came to join me. I almost ordered them back in case I couldn't hold anything and the dark elf was doing something sneaky.

I waited, holding the edge of the forcefield as well. What was going on this time?

I didn't have to wait much longer. The dark elf finally reached forward, his mind coming into contact with mine.

Nuri's presence grew in my mind, the firebird working with me to prevent the dark elf from latching on. It was a strange sensation to have a mental barrier, but it was needed since the dark elf managed to latch on, and I could feel him trying to get into my mind.

With Nuri's help, I pushed him back again, but a second

later, I felt a slap of pain as he took control of the air I had been holding. The air was pulled around as if the dark elf was sucking it in toward the portal.

Frowning and trying to ignore the developing headache, I struck back and stepped closer to the forcefield again. We tussled back and forth. I was in total control then the dark elf snatched something from me to wreck it or suck it into the forcefield.

Every time I stole it back, I noticed it felt more like him and less like the elements on earth usually did. It was disconcerting. But even if the portals were closed, I had a feeling this dark elf could continue this assault if he wished.

But I still didn't understand why. What was he trying to achieve?

I didn't have time to think about it, my mind constantly battling his for what felt like an age while everyone looked on. A couple of times, he managed to get into my head, but I gave him a mental push and shoved him out before he could speak. The last thing I wanted to do was let someone like that into my head if it could be helped.

I was growing tired of the back and forth. Everyone was concerned and trying to save equipment as well as protect people. The elves were with me fighting. I reached out to him near the portal and pushed it back like a person might shove someone through a hole.

It wasn't ideal, but there was suddenly a lot of resistance and another fresh, hard assault directly on my mind. I fought it, using all the techniques I had, but it was a connection and a grip born of threat and frustration. There was little I could do as the dark elf invaded my mind.

*Impressive growth, my dear. But your firebird won't save you forever. I am coming for the world you live in. There's so much fresh and wonderful about it, and all of the elves will be so glad to know they'll be in charge of everything. That I can show them how everything can be theirs. Step aside, and let me show you what can truly be done for our race.*

*No*, I replied, disgusted by what he'd said and how readily he had lied to me and suggested that the elves on this planet would want his rule. I pushed back again, coming in from behind and shoving him as hard as I could and with everything I had left.

It did the trick, pushing him back with such a force and amount of magic that he reeled. A moment later, the portal snapped shut again, and there was an awkward silence.

I looked around at the wreckage around us and the many faces fixed on me. It was clear they were concerned, and I saw that some of them were injured. I had lost sight of everything while I'd been locked in a battle with mostly my mind.

"Was that him?" Minsheng asked.

"Yes. And he wants to hurt this place. He's trying to get me to help him. Or not to stop him."

"Then you should do the opposite," my Shishou replied.

There was no way I could disagree after what had happened. I looked around the portal site at the faces of the elves, humans, and mythicals who needed to remain safe. I was their first hope. And whether Cherisse liked it or not, that meant going to the Mexican portal site and helping defend it.

It also meant training someone to defend the Texan portal. At this rate, the dark elf was going to tear the place apart, and there wasn't going to be anyone here to stop him. Seth seemed to have similar thoughts, however. He came forward with Emily and two other elves I didn't know the names of.

"We're the best single four elementals here," Seth said. "And I think we're going to need to know everything we can about fighting this dark elf."

The young fire elf wasn't wrong, but I wasn't sure I was able to assist them. I did my best anyway, describing everything I could and trying to decide if there was anything else they needed to know.

They were four competent elves and they had the support of others but were underprepared. I felt scared. Whoever this dark elf was, I was pretty sure I was only keeping him at bay because he was working magic on the other side of a portal in a place he couldn't see and where it was attuned more to me than it was to him.

Whichever way you looked at it, it gave me a significant advantage over him and his attempts. Face to face or through an open portal like in Mexico. That was going to be a whole different ball game.

But it made my mind up for me. I was the single most powerful elf on earth. If I didn't stop him from getting onto the planet, then he wasn't going to be stopped.

*I guess we're going to Mexico again,* Zephyr said. *If we are, I insist we get to decide what food they serve us this time.*

As I walked away from the four elves toward Minsheng, I couldn't help but chuckle. I had awesome company.

CHAPTER SIX

Blinking in the evening air, I exhaled. I was riding on
Zephyr's back, Sen curled up asleep in my jacket, and Nuri
and Roth were flying in the large dragon's slipstream. I was
exhausted and had needed to ride for a while, my abilities
drained.

After fighting the dark elf at the Texas site twice in one
day, I hadn't had enough capacity left to fly the whole way.
Of course, Zephyr had assured me that he was more than
capable of flying where we needed, but he was also flag-
ging. We'd flown a lot and had to fight a lot for one day,
not to mention the bonding ceremony and the drama that
went with that.

Finally, I was aware that Nuri hadn't been away from
the Sanctuary since he was reborn, and it was his home. He
said he was okay, but I could feel the tinge of sadness at the
thought of not being back there for a while.

Given I hadn't been afforded the opportunity to talk to
anyone in the Sanctuary about what was happening, who I
was, and everything I was trying to process, I wanted to

sleep there for the night. It would let me talk to the people who mattered and make sure I wasn't missing any information that I'd have had if I'd grown up in the Sanctuary like many other elves.

We landed after dark. The guards waved us forward and let us into the Sanctuary. I was quick to let them know that the council wasn't needed and I was passing through for rest and good conversation. Almost every time I arrived, it was with news or difficulties.

While I had news and things weren't well in the world, it was nothing new and nothing worth dragging them away from much-needed sleep. Especially when I wished for the same.

By the time I reached the guest house we used, however, the four elven masters were there. I was mostly pleased to see them but so tired a part of me wished they had waited until morning.

"We will not keep you from rest long," the air master said, taking in the sight of me. "I'm sure you're tired. But we've collectively been looking at the prophecy and what we know of our elements, and we think some things will help."

I lifted my eyebrows as Aquilan lifted a box and held it out to me.

"Open it in the morning or tonight as you prefer. There's no rush, but I hope it serves you well."

I couldn't take it. Instead, I gaped. I had seen this type of wooden box before.

"Did you make this?" I asked as I finally reached for it, my hand running over carvings similar to the box I'd found Zephyr's egg in.

This made no sense. Amcika had claimed they'd put Zephyr in the warehouse and they'd then sent me the deed to the building in another ornately carved box. How could a third be sitting in front of me?

"None of us made this box. It was one of several Laeroth made when he was honing his skill with wood. He said working with the dead material and having to use it so precisely helped him."

I ran my hands over it before I explained that I owned two and why, realizing that it was a coincidence, but hopefully a sign that what they had given me was something that I was supposed to have. Something that would aid me in meeting this prophecy. For the first time, I found myself wondering if there was possibly some larger force at play.

I'd never believed in fate, and I'd been ignoring talk of a prophecy about me, but maybe something was guiding the Earth, or elves, or the universe. Maybe I had been wrong to ignore it.

"Thank you," I said when I realized they were staring at me.

"No, thank *you*. For giving us hope that we can live through what is almost certainly coming," Bialan replied. "If you have three of Laeroth's creations, we should endeavor to find the fourth."

"There are four of them?" I asked as I placed this one on the table, stroking the ornate lid.

"I believe so," Orthelo said. "But I will get confirmation. They are mentioned a few times in the tales of old. The four greats rarely wasted anything. They knew that one day, another would have to come and finish what they'd started."

It was a lot to take in late at night, but thankfully the elven masters knew they had said enough for now. After promising to talk more in the morning, the four of them left. Sen and Roth were curled up together near the fire, Bialan having kindled it for us and set it ablaze.

Nuri was sitting in the flames, making me raise my eyebrows. However, I could feel no pain coming from the creature, and I was sure that was a good sign that he was fine.

I considered leaving the box, but I couldn't. I was curious and I needed to know if the box was something I was supposed to have or if the contents were.

*Or both*, Zephyr said as he came closer. *There have been many things that we have been given at exactly the right moment.*

It was a good point. It was probably useful for whatever we would face in the future.

With hands shaking from anticipation and fear, I lifted the lid of the box and looked inside. There were several notebooks, some of them in Elvish and some translated stuff. It wasn't going to be information I could work through right away, but I saw a strange dagger in there. I lifted it and noticed the design on the handle. It had vines on up the back of the slightly curved blade.

I picked it up and felt a tingle across the skin of the hand holding it.

*I recognize that*, Zephyr said.

*Nuri too*, the phoenix added.

*It was Laeroth's. It's not one of the great artifacts, but there's something in the gem on the hilt. It helps when you're trying to* grow plants and vines and make them strong or something. And there's a seed in the hilt. It becomes a vine whip.

I lifted my eyebrows and then held it out to Zephyr. He couldn't take it, but he got the gist.

*You seem to prefer to use earth powers, and you know what it can do. I don't need any more funky artifacts, but if something is going to benefit the rest of us, I'm all for passing it to you.*

*If you strap the blade to a horn near the top of my head, I might be able to use it in dragon form,* Zephyr replied.

*But you've never used the powers in dragon form before. Is that possible?*

*I'm not sure, but at worst, it will mean I have it when I morph. And it gives me the chance to try.*

*Good point. And if I strap it up on a horn out of the way, then we'll not lose it or get hurt by it. There's no sheath.*

*There isn't, and it's sharp.*

I grinned and then noticed that the handle had a leather cord attached to it and I could use it to tie it in place.

Zephyr lay down and I climbed up on his back, careful to avoid the horns and spikes farther up his neck. I attached it to the underside of one near the back of his head in the middle and tied it in place.

*How does that feel?* I asked.

*Tingly. I can feel the power in it. I'll test it once we've rested.*

I nodded, disappointed that he wasn't going to do so now, but he had a point. It was late. We needed sleep, and there was no way I was going to get to Mexico in the morning with capacity left if we didn't get some rest soon.

Within minutes, the lid was back on the box, and I was curled up beside Zephyr. I tried to think about everything that was happening and consider some strategies, but I was so tired I fell asleep.

Zephyr moving beside me was the next thing I knew, and I awoke to see the elven masters returning. Bialan noticed the blade strapped to a horn and nodded as he pointed it out.

"You opened the box, then?"

"I did. There is a lot to look through, but I am grateful for everything you do for us. We wouldn't have been able to win half the battles we've fought or achieve half of what we've achieved without everything you have taken the time to teach us and help us with."

The four masters hugged me, then they showed me what they'd brought with them that morning. Breakfast was presented to us—hot, cooked breakfast.

I ate while they talked about the books they'd found and how they could help me. They also spoke more about the boxes and what they might have had in them magic-wise. It was useful information.

When they were done, I told them about my encounters with the dark elf, how they felt, and what he'd tried to do.

"It sounds as if he was probing you and learning you," Aquilan said. "Please be careful. You know much that makes the world vulnerable, and it is said that the dark elf could learn many things from the way he connects. He controls the elements in ways that are far from natural. Where you have had the ability naturally, even if you came by the powers in a strange way, he has fought to claim his against the laws of nature and twisted the elven abilities."

"Like some kind of mental domination?" I asked, the

warning feeling serious but the words seeming to be like something out of a story.

"Not exactly, but similar. He uses brute force, and it gives him access to more than the control and abilities you enjoy. After all, the body is made up of the same things as the rest of the world. And he seems to have a strange ability to read them."

I nodded, not entirely surprised that something like that was possible. If the pillars could take control of the inside of a person and tear them apart, then it made sense that the dark elf could do so. Even the elves in Amcika had fought against the forcefield, and Zephyr had done the same by protecting me when I'd fallen into one.

With the warning made and my understanding of it clear, and the masters getting to their feet again, it was time we left. We had to make our way south to the Mexico portal and find out what was going on, and we couldn't wait forever.

I made sure my bag had everything I needed in it, packing in extra food and water from the Sanctuary, and then made my way along with my bonded mythicals to the southern border of the city. Along the way, we saw elves we recognized and many more who smiled and waved at us. Finally, as we reached the border, I spotted Ronan waiting for us.

Slung on his shoulder was a quiver I'd forgotten I owned, and in his hands was a large modern bow.

"Daisy dropped this off here early this morning. She hasn't woken yet, but your Shishou felt you should have it to head into battle with. And some fresh arrows."

I grinned as I took them and slung them over my shoulders along with everything else I carried. He was right.

"Be careful, Aella," he said as he bowed toward me. "I wish I was going with you this time to aid in defending this land, but I want you not to put yourself in danger beyond the necessary. There are many of us who could yet play a part in this coming fight, and I hope to prepare as many of them as possible in your absence."

"If I can help the elves near the Mexican portal, perhaps it won't be necessary," I replied as I returned the sign of respect.

I wasn't sure how much faith I had in my words, but I preferred it if I was right. As I thought about what was happening with the Texas portal, however, I knew I was unlikely to be right. The dark elf on the other side was pushing hard to find a way through to us. It felt as if it was only a matter of time.

Keeping those fears to myself, I smiled and said goodbye to the elves and centaurs I could see on the border and flew into the air. Sen was riding on Roth's back, curled up tight against the back of his mane and holding on with both hands. Nuri and Zephyr propelled themselves into the air as Roth ran along the ground before soaring upward.

I marveled at them, enjoying the sight of the creatures moving together and knowing that they were a family. We were a family, and I was fighting against the dark elf and those with him as much for their sake as I was anyone else's. I wanted to see them safe and free, not having to risk their lives in the heat of battle alongside me.

Once again, I thought about offering to let them out of

our bond. To give them a chance to be able to do something else and be somewhere else. No sooner had I thought it than I realized I couldn't offer it anymore. Not only did I need them, but I had a feeling the world needed us. If we fell apart or weren't together, the whole world might lose everything.

And then it struck me. At some point in the last few days, I'd finally accepted something important. I was the Henera. And I needed to save the world.

# CHAPTER SEVEN

The mountain loomed in front of us, and I felt sick. I was riding on Zephyr again, the strong dragon soaring effortlessly on a breeze that was carrying us in this direction anyway. It wasn't a sight I liked, this mountain.

So many times, bad things had happened in it. Knowing what I did of being a lab experiment created there made me like it less. I didn't want to be going anywhere near it, but I had little choice. There was danger there that I had to defend against.

On the journey, we'd talked about what we might do depending on what we found. I didn't normally formulate what-if scenarios, preferring to deal with whatever was in front of me, but I didn't expect this situation to be easy to navigate.

The cult living in the mountain had shown arrogance on more than one occasion. They'd made it clear that they thought they were above the rules of not playing with things they didn't understand. And they had displayed the arrogance of thinking they could handle the portal and whatever lay beyond it.

So far, I'd been informed that they couldn't back that confidence up and were struggling. As we approached the mountain, it looked as if they were surviving okay, however.

The military barrier around it had grown and had more soldiers around it, no doubt warned of the threat that the portal represented. Not that I thought it would do them any good. I was pretty sure that the dark elf alone could have mangled every fence and murdered every soldier standing there and not broken a sweat.

It made me wonder what hope I had, but I'd not found a limit to my abilities. Maybe I could grow to beat the dark elf as I was slowly growing to defend against him. If this prophecy was true, that was what I needed to do, keep doing my best to defend and love those around me and learn what I could.

When we were a few miles away, I could see familiar scouts patrolling the skies and the mountain. This was the first time that we didn't hide from any of them. Instead, we kept coming. Zephyr flew lower and made it clear we were aiming for the massive front door that currently stood half-open.

I waved at a scout as we were spotted and they flew our way, air being their element.

"You're not welcome here. Turn back," the male elf said.

I was pretty sure I recognized him from the first large air battle I'd fought with Amcika after they had tried to capture me and force me to open the portal for them. I'd fought with him more than once since then. He wasn't the strongest air elf of the two of us, something I'd proved more than once, and I had to respect him for either the arrogance or bravery that made him challenge me alone.

"I said turn back," he added when I didn't respond.

He flew closer, lifting into a more upright position and hovering a moment.

"I can't. I need to speak to Cherisse, and I am here to help. I'm not a threat, and I want to talk and help defeat the dark elf who still lingers on the other side of the portal."

My words had an effect I wasn't expecting. The elf blinked, nodded, and backed off.

"I'll take you down to the main entrance," he said.

*Maybe they realize they need the Henera,* Zephyr said.

*And all of you. I won't be doing this alone.*

*True, but our power comes from you. The amazing things we can do with the elements aren't possible without you. You give us strength while we help you.*

*However it works, I'm grateful you're on my side and not his.*

As we flew lower, the air elf coming alongside like a stern honor guard, I took deep breaths and quelled the fear in my stomach. I wasn't about to be harmed by anyone in the mountain. I was pretty sure of that. None of them had any reason to, but I was also aware that it wasn't the whole story.

Simon was still an unknown. He'd killed Ascan, for starters. I still didn't know what sort of relationship he had to me. He wasn't a father. The scientific elf had not been part of my life. He'd dumped me at a police station when I was a few days old.

Of course, he'd said that it had been needed. That I wouldn't have bonded with Zephyr and had it stick had I been raised like an elf in the cult. That made me wonder. They had to know that what they were doing was wrong and I wouldn't agree with them. That Zephyr wouldn't agree with them. And that meant Simon was more of an asshole than I'd realized.

It was strange to be so sure of it, but as Zephyr landed and Roth and Nuri joined us, I couldn't help but feel as if I was coming back for a family reconciliation, except I wanted them to apologize, and I wasn't interested in the hugs. He had a lot to apologize and atone for. Assuming it was possible.

As soon as we were on the ground, the air elf nodded to one of the elves on the door, and they came over.

"We'd like to talk to Cherisse about the defense of the portal from hostile forces," I said, borrowing words from the soldiers at the Texas portal site when I'd heard them talking about what was happening.

Again our words had an interesting effect, but this time my direct order was ignored. Instead, the elves looked at me and then at each other and whispered about the situation. I ignored their rudeness since there weren't many people in the cult who had experienced humans and knew what they found rude or not.

Eventually, the elf who had been here a while nodded and broke away. He ran into the building, and the air scout looked at us.

"They won't hurt you, but neither will they be concerned about your safety," the scout said, motioning to the guards flanking the doorway. "It's up to you if you stay."

I wanted to question who he meant by "they," but I was

pretty sure he meant Amcika. The elves in the mountain. It was a strange collective indifference, although there would be some of them who would be curious, or take pity, or want to score points with the Henera by being nice.

Although this was a mountain full of elves, I was sure that elves were an awful lot like humans. We just lived longer and tried to make the most of our powers.

I sat down on the large section of grass to one side, my mythicals joining me, before anyone dared approach, however. They were young and curious, and their eyes kept darting to Nuri. Given how I'd forgotten that I was bonded with another elemental mythical since the last time I'd been in the area and that it meant my fire ability was present, I wasn't sure how to handle it.

I introduced the firebird, wondering if it made much difference to have the name of a creature that could set you ablaze with his talents and skills and not regret a moment of it. It made a positive difference because the elf came bounding closer, not that far from Zephyr.

I made a small fire appear in my hand and bounced it back and forth as if I were juggling it. The elf's eyes went wide and she stumbled, almost falling into Zephyr and me.

I steadied her with air and encouraged her to sit. Then I asked her how she was and began to fill her head with stories of cool things I'd done in battles with the elements I possessed.

"Nothing that fancy," I added as I came to the end of one story. I was getting a numb ass from sitting on the ground, and I was sure that Cherisse had decided to ignore my request.

Before I could get up, however, there was a loud bang,

and the main door swung open slowly. I looked up to see Cherisse and Simon striding out together. I wasn't sure what to do. I'd expected one of them, not both of them. Anger flared in me at seeing the man who had killed Ascan. He hadn't cared.

Cherisse strode over to me, her eyes flashing with anger.

"Get off my mountain," she said with no hint of fear or compassion for me.

I glanced at Simon as I felt her take control of the water around her to deter me. Simon had the good sense to look down and gulp.

"Is it *your* mountain?" I asked. "If we're honest about everything going on and who I am now, surely this is as much my mountain. Assuming it's not overrun by the dark elf's forces."

I didn't do more than solidify the usual air barrier around my body, aware that an overt defense might look like I was preparing for an attack.

"How dare you? You've not once made an effort to treat this place as your—"

I lifted my hand as she spoke, feeling her anger rise and the water in the air and ground start to pull tighter together as she prepared to throw it at me. Taking control of it from her, I simply held it in the air.

"I'm not here to threaten you. Or to steal it from you. All I am here to do is to help. I know you had a hand in making me. And I know you made me so I could open that portal you have active, but if I understand everything correctly, you did so because you thought I could protect and defend against this dark elf if he did still live."

"We have no confirmation he's still alive," Cherisse replied, her teeth gritted.

While she spoke, I could feel her mind carefully probing for the water I'd taken. As quickly as I'd snatched it, I let it go. Some of it fell out of the air like rain that pattered, but if I was going to get her to trust me, I had to show I didn't want to hurt her, just defend myself.

Her eyes widened as she took control again. I didn't make another move, letting her process what had happened.

"Someone showed up at the Sanctuary. Said that you'd had a lot of trouble with the portal. Why don't you tell me about it?" I said.

"There's nothing we can't handle. We've trained for this our whole lives. We know what we're doing."

I wanted to remind her that I'd trained for this as well, mostly thanks to her elves and the way they had hunted me, kidnapped me, and then tried to kill me before realizing they needed me again, luring me step-by-step into the mountain once more, and then putting my life on the line so Zephyr would open the portal. Or how they'd killed one of my allies and friends.

I had every reason to hate them and leave them to their fate. Yet here I was, not wanting the rest of the world to be put in danger. Not wanting them to die. I'd wanted to hate Simon at first. And I still didn't like him, his methods, and the life he was willing to snuff out, nor what they'd done to make me, but I'd been making a family of my own with the mythicals I had bonded with. I'd grown that with my Shishou and many of the people in the warehouse.

I had a family. As much as I'd always hoped to find parents who loved me, I had a family that did the same.

"You haven't found what you were hoping to find on the other side, have you?" I asked when we continued to stand in a stalemate, still not leaving.

Cherisse had begun to turn away, but she looked in my direction again. "What we've found or not is none of your business."

"I know this can't be easy on you. I know you had hopes. I am offering my help to defend this home of yours, even if it's not mine. To defend the elves here I know you care about. Let me help you. I'm not asking you for anything else. I don't need to go through the portal, close it, or have any agenda for its use. Just help defend this planet and this mountain from a force none of us is ready for."

I thought Cherisse was going to give in and Simon even stepped forward, his eyes softer and his expression implying that he agreed with me. I was surprised that he was on my side, but I wasn't going to complain about finding unexpected allies. Even if it was someone I still very much wanted to punch or worse every time I thought about Ascan.

"You say you want to help, but I know what you really mean. You want to be the one in control. The one making the decisions and working out who gets to do what and where. I've heard the stories. I know how you boss everyone around and dictate what's going to happen to everyone around you."

I lifted my eyebrows, not sure I understood the attack on me. There had been times I had given commands, but they were almost always in the heat of battle or related to one. No one had yet told me anything that would match with the dictatorial behavior I was being accused of. At least, I didn't think something like that had happened.

The moment I accepted that it might have happened, I started thinking back through my conversations and the times I'd told someone else what to do. There had been more battles than I could remember, although a lot of them had been with very few of us. Had I offended someone? Made someone feel controlled and unappreciated?

*There's only one person who could have told her something like that, even if it's not true. Chris,* Zephyr said. *And anything he thinks of us will be colored by how we asked him to leave.*

I wished I'd been gentler with the part-gnome. I was mortified that even with a twisted perspective, he could confidently say that I had been controlling.

"I mean it. I want to help. Let me prove it. Kick me out again if you prove right. I can't take the whole mountain on alone. I can't force my way in, and I can't stay unbidden."

Although there was a chance I could fight the elves, as long as there weren't too many at once and especially if a bunch of them had been fighting the dark elf or his forces through the portal, I didn't plan on saying that.

Instead, I looked calm and non-threatening. Somehow I had to convince Cherisse.

"No," she said, her eyes meeting mine, ablaze with fiery determination. "You will never be welcome in my mountain. You're not my Henera."

I frowned, trying to think of something else to say, but I

got the impression that it would be futile. Her mind was made up, and there was nothing I could do.

Nodding, I took a step back. I'd tried, but I wasn't going to force the issue.

"I'll be nearby for a few days," I said before a loud clap of thunder sounded above us.

I looked up as Cherisse swore. Something was up there, and it was not happy. I heard the familiar sounds of elven battle, although they were faint, as if it were happening a long way off.

Without another word to me, Cherisse hurried into the mountain, many of the elves sweeping after her.

*We have to help*, I said to Zephyr, hoping he had some ideas about what to do.

*We can fly in from the top*, he replied and spread his wings.

Scooping up Sen, I sent encouragement to Nuri and Roth to do the same. Within seconds, we were in the air and flying up the side of the mountain, heading for danger and the sounds of battle.

# CHAPTER EIGHT

As we came closer to the top of the mountain, I flew over to Zephyr, then landed on his back and let him carry me into battle. I could fly easily, even high on the mountain, but I wanted to save my energy. I wished I'd eaten more when we'd stopped to wait outside the base of the mountain, but there was nothing that could be done about that now.

Roth struggled to keep up, the flying water pegasus able to run and power through the surf far faster than on land. Although I felt sorry for him, he would have to join us in the battle as he could.

I took in the scene as we finally rose above the portal and the gap in the rock we could get through and then down toward the shimmering light. It was active, a circle of swirling colors that was never still and somehow not quite there. Feeling sick looking at it, I focused away from it.

Around the portal were elves, but their skin was a different color. Where the elves on earth had skins of various colors and tans, as humans did, I was pretty sure that the elves coming through the portal hadn't been anywhere near a color like the humans before. They had dark skin that was purple in tone.

Both males and females had shaggy manes of thick black hair and wore very little, their bodies adorned with almost rag-like clothing.

One thing they had in common with us, however, was the ability to control the elements. They were flinging air, water, fire, plants, and rocks around as if they were always controlled by the incoming elves.

Going unnoticed gave me the opportunity to study them, looking for a weakness or a person in charge that I might be able to deter and then break the will of the group.

There didn't appear to be a leader, and I noticed that they were all wearing blank expressions. Were these mind-less drones? I had no idea, but they fought relentlessly, and Cherisse was still making her way up the mountain.

*We need to help*, I thought to the others as I encouraged Zephyr downwards. He furled his wings enough to drop us through the gap in the cave roof, and I helped him slow to land gracefully to one side.

We drew attention, and I could feel elves trying to take control of the air that held my barrier in place. I resisted, finding the group that was closest and most focused on me to be fighting hard. They finally made noise, showing they weren't mindless drones, but I couldn't understand them. It was as if they'd spoken in an entirely strange language.

Of course, they might have, but it wouldn't make them any more likely to win our mental duel. It was time to show them this planet belonged to us.

Sen jumped out of my jacket as soon as Zephyr landed and pulled out her little dart gun. At the same time, Roth activated the device he had for helping him focus his water. At this altitude, there was plenty of moisture in the air, and I could feel it being sucked into Roth to help fuel him.

Taking control of air and raising the gloves I was given, I blasted dark elves off their feet, aiming for any that looked as if they had the upper hand. It wasn't a perfect solution to the problem, but it distracted everyone and gave the elves defending the mountain a chance to regroup.

It was clear that they had been struggling, the dark elves having formed an efficient pattern of abilities and positions and pushing forward.

I counted about forty of them as I stepped closer and blasted one straight back and into the swirling vortex that the portal appeared to be made of.

*That won't have killed them, will it?* I asked Zephyr, fearing it was a one-way thing and not something you could walk either way through unless you dialed out or something.

*I don't believe so. It will make him very confused. It can take a while to travel through the portal, and it is thought that without mental preparation, it can be confusing. I confess that I appreciate the effectiveness of the tactic and can only support it with these silent killing machines.*

Feeling Zephyr's request for an adventurer to go into battle with, I pulled up my sleeves and reached into the ground to create a spot that would keep me steady. It wasn't ideal, but I touched the first rock as someone tried to hit me with an air blast. When I looked around, I saw three dark elves who had come together to attack me.

I gave them my attention as vines shot overhead and smacked one of them off their feet.

*The blade works*, I heard Zephyr say.

I blinked before chuckling and noticing it had dropped seeds as it had grown, flowers forming along it at lengths. I grabbed hold of the seeds, momentarily stunned by how much information and life was packed into each one. Then I hurled the vines forward as they grew and I repeated what I had seen as a battle tactic.

My strike wasn't as effective as Zephyr's, but it stung the hand of the middle dark elf, who stepped back as if he had been hit mentally. I internally whooped with delight. If the feisty dark elves were able to be beaten this easily, I might have the chance to help Zephyr become familiar with his dagger and learn what it could do.

Having pushed back more, I noticed Cherisse and Simon turn up, flinging their abilities around. Simon flew closer, hit by an air blast that was meant for me.

He wobbled and smacked his head on an outcrop of rock. I almost ignored him, but having defended elves a lot recently, my reflexes kicked in. I cushioned him with air, stopped him from spinning, and helped him back to a stable position, all while flinging air around.

By the time Zephyr had landed and had a breather, there was a thank you from Simon, and I moved on to the next target. I tried not to think about how I'd probably saved the life of an elf who didn't deserve it. For the moment, he had been an ally, and I couldn't let my desire for consequences for him stop me from saving this planet.

Cherisse joined the fray, close to Roth and the water he was cannoning out. They worked together naturally, although I suspected Cherisse wasn't aware of the pegasus near her, making it easier on her and giving her more water to work with.

If I was vindictive, I'd have pushed the water out and toward her so that she noticed she was being aided, but I didn't. Instead, I focused on the dark elves nearest me, hitting them with air as Simon did the same. Between us, we kept them from being able to recover.

After sending another dark elf back through the portal, another ten rushed out of the swirling opening.

*Let me breathe on them*, Zephyr said. *Can you hold it around the portal?*

*Yes, go for it*, I replied, noticing that the cult elves couldn't get that close. It was a perfect idea, and I was annoyed that we hadn't thought of it. I blasted another elf with one hand as I looked at Zephyr. I moved out of the way for Sen to shoot her dart gun at another enemy before she bounded off again and I avoided a blast of water from someone else.

I was tempted to grab the rush of water and send it back, but it would have distracted me from what I needed to be doing.

As Zephyr exhaled, his breath weapon billowing out toward the portal, I took control. It reached a couple of dark elves, their eyes going wide before they clutched at their throats and then collapsed. They hadn't been ready for an attack like that.

Feeling emboldened, I took the gas and moved the cloud closer to the attackers. Before the ten or so on the platform in front of the portal could react to the carnage they were seeing, let alone the threat that a fairly normal-looking cloud represented, I had enveloped them with it and most of them were knocked out.

I focused and held it there, feeling the bodies of the dark elves inside as they fell back and were paralyzed. It wasn't ideal since they were still on this side of the portal, but the vines spread out and lifted them. They were tossed back into the other dimension or whatever it was.

With the reinforcements dealt with and the current group finally being overwhelmed and pushed back, their numbers reduced as well, I was calmer. I stopped worrying about hitting them before they hit me and focused on draining their powers. I was getting good at distracting them by taking control of the elements around them and making them think I was going to use it against them. They then wasted energy trying to claim it from me while I simply melted away to take control of something else.

I spotted Chris fighting. He was using a gadget in his hand to read something. I was distracted, thinking about what he could be doing this close to danger. Of course, I hadn't expected him to help in battle directly.

Finally, he was satisfied, and he backed up from the portal and put the device away, no longer having a purpose in the fight. I wondered if he'd noticed me until our eyes met. He gave me a slow up and down of his head before slinking off the raised area near the portal.

I was hit with a blast of water, my body drenched and cold before I remembered what was going on. I was supposed to be fighting these dark elves, not getting distracted by gnomes I'd once thought were family and had my back.

Of everything I'd been through, that felt as if it was one

of the worst personally—Chris deciding that he supported Amcika and their plans more than me.

*You can hit him with an air blast later*, Zephyr pointed out, the vine from his head whipping forward again and cracking where an elf had been the moment before. The elf was so startled that he hesitated, and Simon knocked him off his feet. Before he could get up, Roth drenched him, and I picked him up and hurled him through the portal.

I was soon looking for the next target, but there was only a handful of dark elves still standing. As if they too realized that, they threw up an air barrier and retreated behind it, pulling it back with them and trying to deflect anything that came their way.

Although I considered hitting them some more and draining them, there wasn't much point in draining myself to gain a temporary victory. That said, I noticed the elves around me didn't give up, Simon leading a charge forward that trapped one more of the dark elves and had them paralyzed by Zephyr's gas weapon.

Feeling tired for so many reasons, I stopped where I was and let go of everything but the usual air barrier that wound around my body. Zephyr came closer, resting his head near my shoulder. I reached up and stroked his scales, the familiar smoothness providing comfort.

The battle we'd fought had grown easier as more elves had arrived to help, but I had gotten the impression that we were being tested. As if this was true, I noticed the vortex spin tighter, and then I could feel the control of a powerful dark elf coming through.

I stepped closer, trying to force the control back. If anything, it alerted the dark elf to my presence. He latched onto me, and I struggled against it for several seconds before Nuri landed on my shoulder.

*And you're here as well, my dear. You do get around. I hope you stay for the show. There's going to be a lot of action, but it's a shame you can't be in two places at once. You're missing my plans for the other portal.*

My blood ran cold, the words buzzing around my head.

*Fight, Henera,* Nuri said, breaking through the panic before it could fully form. *Distracting. Probing all of us.*

The warning was enough to make me push back against the connection. Nuri was right. I was letting the dark elf probe at my thoughts and bonds, the dull pain growing as his reach did. With Nuri's help and walking back from the chaos and portal, I managed to reduce the connection and break it entirely, attacking it from the side.

I breathed with relief, but it would be short-lived if I didn't push back the control farther. Knowing this last part was harder, I did everything I could to focus. Simon came closer, my mind aware of him, but he wasn't there to talk to me or distract me. Instead, he joined in the struggle.

Together we battled the control in the air and more elves stepped up, forming a line with us at the center. I could feel the dark elf pushing back, trying to connect with another elf now and then, but every time he did, I struck, snapping his connection and stopping him from forming another.

I could feel myself growing more drained, the effort of fighting the dark elf far more than I'd ever expected, especially after flying to the portal and fighting off the dark elf minions he'd pushed through toward us.

I wasn't alone battling the dark elf this time, however. Although some elves stepped back, spent, Simon, Cherisse, and many other of the stronger elves remained, pushing back the control until he withdrew, taking everything but the vague awareness of his presence in the elements around us.

Exhaling, I felt tired in a way I never had before. As if I'd been fighting panic and anxiety, my mental capacity almost entirely used up. Whatever the dark elf was and however he had come about his powers, it was unnatural, and it was far different from any fight I'd ever been in before.

As I looked around me, I noticed I wasn't the only one struggling. So many elves had sat down or fallen where they stood. Cherisse was bent over, resting her hands on her thighs, and Simon was panting.

"How often is that happening?" I asked Simon, the nearest to me.

"At least twice a day. Sometimes more."

"You really need my help."

"Yes. Yes, we do." Simon spoke and looked at Cherisse as he did.

She glanced between us, having heard every word, but she didn't speak. I expected her to express her objection at any point, but as she straightened, she fixed her gaze on my face.

"You answer to us, and you help where you're told to help. And your mythicals pull their weight too," she said eventually.

"As long as we are treated with respect and dignity, we'll cooperate. We find ourselves on the same side. We can live with that and fight against our new common enemy."

This satisfied Cherisse. She nodded curtly and walked off, giving commands for the area to be resecured.

I exhaled once more and leaned into Zephyr and his warm scales. We'd done it. For now, we were part of the team defending against the dark elf. That meant getting food and rest.

*Let's go find out if anyone here knows how to make a decent pizza*, I said to my mythicals, hearing several of them chuckle in response.

We'd be okay, but this was going to be one tough fight.

# CHAPTER NINE

Sitting in the strange room that passed as a mess hall in the mountain was a whole new experience for me and my mythicals. It was clear that many of the elves were curious about us, especially about the bonds and the mythicals.

Unlike at the Sanctuary, where there were plenty of interesting creatures running around, here I was the only elf with a mythical, let alone four. On top of that, there was a system for who got to eat when. I'd not only broken that system by accident, but Zephyr and Roth ate a lot, and Sen and Nuri had some interesting dietary requirements.

The whole thing had taken a long time to sort out before we could eat, and by then, I had been lightheaded and starving. It hadn't been an ideal way to start our life in the mountain. I was pretty sure some of the hungry elves around us were wishing we weren't around.

If we were going to help the elves defend their home, I needed to eat. We'd have to make it easier for everyone to accommodate us.

I missed Daisy and Minsheng and the elves I was

normally with. Mealtimes with them were my favorite times of the day. I hoped they were working to help keep the Texas portal safe and we were helping the world most by being apart from each other.

As soon as we'd eaten, we made our way out of the canteen and away from the tense atmosphere. Zephyr had taken human form, the inside of the mountain not designed to accommodate him in dragon form, and he slipped his fingers into mine as we found ourselves stared at and whispered about by yet another group of elves.

There were elves everywhere, far more inside the strange rock home than we'd ever realized. It was a strange position to be in. Of course, I'd been inside the mountain before. And I'd fought many of the elves. I recognized some of them from past battles, but the weirdness was fueled by their reaction to our presence.

I ignored it and instead asked the nearest elves which floor we could find Simon and Cherisse on to discuss how we could help. No one wanted to tell me where the latter was, citing that the cult leader didn't like being disturbed and that she summoned you if she wanted you. That left us with Simon, someone we wanted to talk to and also wanted to give a solid beating. Everyone either had no clue who he was or just that he worked in the labs.

With nowhere else to go and no idea where else to report for duty, Zephyr urged me to go find Simon.

*I have no idea what to say to him about creating me*, I said to Zephyr as my finger hesitated over the elevator button.

*I know, but he still had a hand in making you. And he might know who your mother was. Or the woman who bore you. It's something, but I won't push you to do so if you're not ready. I'll hold your hand and stand with you. No matter what you find out about who you are and where you've come from, you're still our bonded elf. I still love you for who you've become and who you are.*

Zephyr's words helped calm me. I was brave enough to push the button and go to find Simon. If nothing else, I wasn't alone. Whatever I was facing, my bonded mythicals were gladly facing it with me.

Warm affection was radiating off them. Nuri was new to our group but already felt like one of the family. With any luck, we'd also find out more about how our bonds worked and how our entire group was possible. Anything that might help us feel more connected to each other or help us when fighting.

Part of me didn't want to put my anger at Simon for what he'd done aside. I wanted to pound him into oblivion and make him pay for the pain he'd caused. I also knew I'd fought alongside him. I'd saved his life, and he'd helped fight off the dark elf. Somehow he'd become an ally.

As we reached one of the lab floors and got out of the elevator, I noticed that this one was a lot quieter than many of the other floors had been. There were some small bedrooms off to one side, most of their doors open and the beds unoccupied, but that wasn't entirely surprising at this time of day. I hurried past them, looking for the elf who had made me.

I both hoped to find him and didn't as I checked laboratories next, the first full of plants being studied. Once again, I hurried on.

The third large lab room gave me what I sought. Simon stood at a large microscope, looking at something under it.

He either heard something or sensed my presence in the air because he looked straight up and at me.

"Aella, Henera, come in. I hope you've eaten and rested since the fight?" As he asked the question, he glanced at the desk nearby. It had a tray with a couple of empty plates on it, showing he'd also made sure to eat, but he hadn't had to go to the canteen for it. I hesitated by the door, not sure I wanted to get any closer to him, but I couldn't stand out in the hallway.

Slowly I moved into the room, my mythicals coming too and Zephyr's hand never leaving mine. I was tired and anxious, the tenseness in my body making me ache. Simon glanced my way again before going back to the microscope. It was then that I realized he'd asked me a question.

"I'm rested," I said. "But no one anticipated my mythicals and me getting to eat. I think I accidentally broke a rule or two."

Simon chuckled and looked my way again before moving his stool away from the microscope.

"You're the Henera; you're not made for rules. I'll make sure you're assigned a decent room on the best floor and have your food brought to you."

I lifted an eyebrow; that was going to ruffle some feathers. I considered opening my mouth to refuse, but Zephyr's mental negative made me stop. This conversation wasn't going where I'd expected.

*You think it's a good idea?* I asked Zephyr while I composed myself again.

*I think the benefits outweigh the negatives. We get somewhere we can run away to and be alone, and we don't have to fit in with everyone if they're not going to accept us anyway. There are other ways to get people to see that we're just another set of mythicals than eating with them, especially when Roth and I eat far more than is allowed.*

I exhaled, noticing Simon was staring at me, his eyes narrower than before. Did he realize we were talking in our heads?

"Thank you," I replied, trying to sound as normal as possible despite his scrutiny putting me on edge. "That would be helpful."

"Fantastic. Consider it done, but I get the feeling that's not why you've come to find me here."

"No." I shook my head as I tried not to think about the memory of him killing Ascan and instead to think about the best way to phrase my question. "I want to know more about me. About my creation and why you did this. I want to understand what I am."

Simon frowned but nodded. "I can understand you wanting to know that. I don't have many answers for you, however. We created you because we created you. We used magic for a lot of it. And we did it because we knew you would one day open the portals and either defeat the dark elf of old or find him dead."

"I knew all that already."

"I don't know what you expect from me. It wasn't some big ritual or magic ceremony. I spliced some DNA together and used magic to ensure that you were viable and would have access to all the elements."

"At least tell me who my mother was." My fists clenched, and I instinctively reached to control the air and earth around me.

"Your mother. You don't have a mother."

"You had someone give birth to me. There's an elf somewhere who acted as my mother for at least a few months."

Simon's frown deepened, and I could tell that he was thinking about his next words carefully. I wanted to shake him and get my answers, but I gave him a moment.

"There was a woman. We had to keep her sedated most of the time and prevent her body from rejecting you. I don't remember much about her. She gave birth to you when the time came."

"What was her name? Where is she now?"

"I don't know her name. I was never told, and I never asked. None of us did."

"You don't know her name?" I demanded as I twirled the air around us, my anger coming out of me in waves. "I want to know her name. I want to find her."

"You can't. She's not alive anymore." Simon got up, feeling the anger and what I was doing to the air. He had the sense not to challenge my control, however. We both knew I was far stronger than he was. But there was also a strange grin on his face as he looked around at the swirling air and everything beginning to flutter and move.

I tensed even more. How could every avenue and every bit of hope I had that I'd meet someone involved in my creation who might care about me end in death or nothing but the cult's arrogant plans and their attempts to play god and decide the fate of two planets?

*Careful, Aella,* Zephyr said. *As much as I want to punch the smug look on this guy's face into next week, he is probably the biggest reason we're here defending this portal and not kicked back out of the mountain.*

Zephyr was right, but that didn't mean I liked it. Taking a deep breath, I thought through what I'd been told and what I was going to do about it. I wanted to punch this guy or turn him upside down in a spinning vortex and fling him around like a spinning top until he puked or passed out. I had no idea what that would do to my ability to stay, however.

As I thought about Minsheng, Daisy, and everyone else, I knew that I couldn't do anything to risk the position I had gained. Cherisse didn't want me in the mountain, and I was pretty sure she wasn't the only elf who felt that way. My skills might be more needed than everyone here realized, but until they accepted it, I had to be the bigger person.

"Is there a grave or a marker or something?" I asked, not knowing where else to go with my desire to have some closure.

"No. She would have been incinerated. As all the rejected elves were when they died."

"Rejected elves?" I snapped.

"After giving birth to you and trying to go back to her duties in the mountain, she went insane. Tried to kill several elves, including Cherisse and me. She had to be dealt with, and there was nothing left when it was done."

I gaped at Simon's cool, almost detached composure as he described what had happened to the woman who had given birth to me.

*We can find a way to mourn her and honor her memory together,* Zephyr said. *I know that won't take away your pain now. But we'll take what we do know of her and honor her in some way. I promise.*

Zephyr's arm tightened around my waist as he spoke, making me feel calmer. It also reminded me that we had another purpose for finding Simon. Zephyr needed answers as well.

"It seems there is little you either want or can tell me, but I hope you know more of Zephyr's story. He remembers a mother. What happened to her? And why did you put him in the warehouse when you did?"

Here Simon perked up. He got up and went over to a small row of journals on a shelf. Pulling out one of them, he had a quick flick through.

"Your mother. She was an impressive dragon, Zephyr," Simon said. "But she gave your egg up to us gladly."

"She did?" Zephyr and I asked together.

"Yes. She was being hunted by the agency as it was then. And we came across her once they'd wounded her. She gave us your egg, hoping that it would mean you would one day bond with an elf. I was sure enough that I could promise her that when the agents turned up, she fought them to the death so all of us could get away with your egg and everything we needed to make Aella."

I frowned as I studied Simon. He appeared to be telling the truth, but it was hard to tell for sure. I wanted to believe him for Zephyr's sake, but at the same time, it seemed as if it was the sort of thing the cult members might say to keep us happy with them. Not that all of them wanted to keep us happy. And if he truly wanted that, he wouldn't have told me so much that was disappointing.

"Why didn't you keep us both here if you were so sure we'd bond and Aella was the Henera?" Zephyr asked, his human form body tensing as well.

"Because your genetic memories would have made you hate us. Your bond would have been broken by you the moment you realized Aella was Amcika had she grown up here and had you been born here."

"He wouldn't have given me a chance to get to know him because he'd have hated what I'd have been brainwashed into?" I asked.

"Yes, that was a possibility we couldn't have entertained, and we were right to make that call. You've shown a lack of desire to even begin to understand us."

I opened my mouth to retort about understanding their delusional belief that they could speak for all humanity and elvenkind perfectly well, but Zephyr squeezed me and then stepped forward as he let go of me.

"I have no idea if my mother was right to trust you or not. Or if you're telling the truth, but I do know one thing for sure. It is an honor to be bonded with Aella. Not because she's Henera, or powerful, or something unique and created by elves. But because she has a heart. She has empathy and understanding. She's brave and determined. She's everything that Amcika lacks and badly needs if it wants to be a force for good in the world. And most of all, she's not willing to murder other elves just to get what she wanted."

Simon looked at us, and the smug smile reappeared on his face.

"I am glad you've found you can respect each other. And I am truly grateful you're here now, even if I think you could be less judgmental. I did what I needed to, even with the elf who betrayed us and began helping you. His death served its purpose in the great prophecy. However, if you've finished making demands of me and churning up my laboratory with your powers, I have work to do. We have a dark elf to fight, and I'm sure you'll appreciate my help as much as I am grateful for yours."

I heard the tell-tale growl from Zephyr that made it clear he didn't appreciate being dismissed in such a way, but this time I reached for him with my hand and mind to calm him. It was time to leave and rest. At any moment, we might need to fight the dark elf again, and for that, we needed clear minds.

# CHAPTER TEN

As we were shown into the new room Simon had arranged for us, I gasped. There was a wonderful view of the surrounding land, and the room was far larger than any we'd ever been in. I slowly walked toward the window as Roth, Nuri, and Sen explored the room behind me.

I tried not to think about how unfair it was that we had a room this large when many of the elves in the mountain had tiny rooms and no windows or natural light. I'd seen many of the rooms, and none of them had looked as good as this one.

There was a four-poster bed big enough that Zephyr would have been able to curl up on it in dragon form if he'd wanted to. And he could take dragon form in the room. On top of the space to spread out, there was a fireplace and some books and food laid out for us. Bread, fruit, and cheese sat on a large platter in the middle of a dining table.

With it were drinks and everything Nuri, Roth, and Sen needed, including dirt, a perch, and a large shallow basin of water that appeared to have a small stream babbling through it.

The combination of everything hewn into the natural rock of the mountain was stunning. Had this not been the heart of a cult, I'd have been happy. As it was, I still appreciated it.

Before I could do more than pick up an apple and bite into it, there was the sound of a knock on the door. Roth hurried over to it, the water pegasus closer than the rest of us. He opened it as I noticed I had instinctively taken control of the air and rock around me again.

There was an elf I recognized on the other side. One of the elves who had guarded my cell the very first time I'd been here. His eyes bulged as he looked around the room. I picked up another apple and offered it to him, going over to the door as I invited him in.

"I can't stay," he said, but he took the fruit. "The portal is active again. Cherisse thinks they can handle it, but I know what you can do, and Simon told me I had to make sure you always knew."

"Thank you. Simon is right," I replied as I rushed past the elf and into the corridor. Feeling rather than seeing the others come after me, I hurried down toward the elevator. We were several floors above and off to one side of the portal, but I wasn't sure of the quickest way to get there. There was no way I wasn't showing up to help either.

Zephyr caught up to me, Sen with him. Nuri flew and landed on my shoulder as I hit the button to call the elevator. Nothing happened.

"They've started switching it off in emergencies," the elf called from behind. "You'll have to take the stairs."

Swearing under my breath, I rushed to where the stairs were, hoping it would be easier to get through to them than it usually was. Thankfully there was an earth elf I recognized there with several other elves around her, boring through the rock.

I started helping her, taking control of a section she had been neglecting to make a wider gap. She glanced my way as I reached her side, and I thought I saw her flinch, then look around us.

"Sorry. Didn't mean to startle you." I smiled at her. "Thought it would get us there quicker if I helped."

"We're not supposed to waste our powers," she replied. "Cherisse said only one earth elf was supposed to do this on each floor."

"Great. I'm Henera, and Simon has informed me that I don't have to follow the rules if I think I can help and manage my abilities. I'm getting to the point that my air and earth are pretty long-lasting. So let's get to the fight and make sure we're not overrun."

I thought I saw a grin flash across the girl's face before she went back to the job, and we soon had a gap wide enough that the elves could rush through. I hesitated, not wanting to get in their way but not wanting to hurry them to danger ahead of me and look as if I wasn't willing to brave it.

Zephyr soon slipped through and hurried along with Sen on his shoulder. Nuri stayed on mine, and I slipped into the stairwell as the opportunity arose. As I went inside, another couple of elves came running down. One was holding a floating fireball that lit their way. I copied them and gathered the last few of the elves and Roth to me.

The earth elf who had opened the stairwell with me came last.

"I need to close it," she said. "Go on. I'll be okay in the dark."

I hesitated.

"I'll stay with her," Zephyr said. "Go join the fight and light everyone else."

I didn't want to leave Zephyr behind, but I didn't want to argue. Anything could be happening at the portal site, and we might be needed.

After a moment of hesitation, I hurried down the stairs with the group of elves, winding around as we went. We lit openings up as elves came pouring out and joined us, and other earth elves were reclosing the gap. I helped where I could, trying not to delay but making sure many got there as soon as possible.

As soon as another fire elf joined us, I sent the majority of the group ahead with them and waited for the stragglers myself. I could feel Zephyr as he started moving again and then I rushed full pelt down the last few sections of steps to the correct floor.

On the portal floor the opening was wider, allowing elves to flow in from above and below the largest floor. There weren't as many as I expected, but there were a lot of the powerful elves—the ones who had fought hard and chased me in the past.

I didn't react to the knowledge that I was once an enemy of these elves but focused on the task. There was a stream of elves heading to the portal site, but again, not as many as I'd have expected. That said, we hadn't rested fully since the last attack, and very few others would have either.

Simon appeared, running faster with his wind ability as I rounded the corner to the portal. There were many dark elves around it, hurling water, rocks, plants, and fire and making the air move in strange ways. The elves were struggling to do anything but defend themselves, and I could see that several were hurt, burned, sporting bruises and gashes, or wrapped in the vines they were fighting.

I took control of the air and earth around the portal and in the large open cavern. Things calmed, and the dark elves reeled back. I hit the fire and water elves with a blast of air as I shook the ground underfoot, then I was bombarded by minds wanting to take control.

It was the respite the cult elves needed, however. They gathered themselves, and Cherisse glared at me as she barked orders. I shook my head as Simon and Zephyr came to stand on either side of me.

*Focus on the dark elves and pushing them back*, Zephyr said. *Cherisse can sulk at us after we've saved everyone.*

I grinned and did just that, working with Simon, Zephyr, Roth, Sen, and Nuri to hurl the elements at dark elves and either knock them out or push them back until they were forced to retreat through the portal.

Although I'd quickly turned things around and there were more elves to fight back and defend the mountain, there were also more dark elves coming through and it felt as if for every one we sent back to the other planet, two came rushing at us.

I was hit by elements. Roth was blocking fire with his water, and Nuri swallowed a fireball at one point. Zephyr used the elements as swiftly and accurately as I did, and Simon kept blasting anything off its feet that was so much as aimed in his direction.

*We need to turn this tide and push them back*, I said to Zephyr as I saw another Amcika elf running out of capacity and backing off from the fight to pass out.

This wouldn't go well if we didn't do something soon. Despite my words to Zephyr, I wasn't panicked. Although the numbers weren't larger than any other quantity of elves I'd fought in the past, they were formidable and more powerful. But I noticed that some of the earliest dark elves to come through and fight were beginning to wane. I was tired, but I wasn't hurting, and Zephyr still felt pretty good.

Eating had helped us recharge and made it easier to fight. I was also pretty sure I recognized some of the dark elves who were fighting us, who had been in the wave of combatants in the attack when I'd arrived at the mountain.

If that was true, they would also not be at full capacity.

As I was hit with a wind blast that almost knocked me off my feet, I let myself be pushed back as I rebalanced myself and had a look around. This wasn't the number of elves I'd expected on our side. Far more Amcika had fought against me and the elves from the Sanctuary when I had been escaping. This wasn't the full power of the mountain.

"Where is everyone?" I asked Simon. "We need some reinforcements."

"Cherisse doesn't want us all defending at once. Some have to rest after each battle."

"Not if it means we lose," I replied.

Simon couldn't respond, a vine snatching at his leg and pulling him off his feet. I caught him with air and fought the control of the vine around his ankle, taking it into my mind and then unwrapping it from his limb. I then flicked it back toward the initial controller, pulling them off their feet with the plant they'd created.

With a quick motion, I used it to hurl them through the portal.

*Another one down*, I thought before Zephyr did something similar with the dark elf beside.

The repeated action inspired the earth elves around us, who joined in growing vines and flinging dark elves around as if they were nothing but dolls. I winced when a few were flung off-target and smacked into rock or the stumps of the old pillars to either side. Most went limp, not returning to the fight, but some cried out in pain as limbs were broken or worse.

I helped the elves struggling, feeling bad even for the dark elves we fought. I never liked hurting others in ways that couldn't be healed or fixed. The fights were so often pointless.

More elves appeared through the portal, but I noticed some of them were elves we'd sent back at the beginning of the battle. It seemed there was either a delay in the travel time or they weren't coming back right away. With no way to know for sure, I had to wonder if they were reporting what had happened to someone on the other side.

Like the previous time, I hadn't felt the presence of the main dark elf. If he was monitoring this fight, he was doing so from the other side of the portal and not trying to feel for the elements on this side.

As more elves joined us, called up by Cherisse to replace the elves who were exhausted, I knew we would finally push back this group. While the others were doing that, I changed my attention to the portal. I had waited every time for something to connect with me. What if I reached through? Could I explore the other side with my mind?

Not sure but feeling well enough to try, I let Zephyr know what I was doing and worked my way to the edge of the battle and into the shadows so I could concentrate. I took several deep breaths.

As soon as I was calmer, I moved forward with my mind, reaching into the portal. Something grabbed my presence and tried to pull it through like a string unraveling in my head. I winced since it stung and hoped my mythicals weren't feeling it the way I was, but there was nothing I could do now. My mind was rushing toward the other side.

When I emerged, it was like taking a deep breath after holding it underwater. It was as if I were exploring a room. I connected to the air first, tentatively reaching out. I recognized the control of the dark elf, his marker on the elements. They resisted me.

His mind was somewhere else, and the only movement was the reappearance of other dark elves as they were sent back through the portal and into the room. Most of them either collapsed or hurried away.

I continued to reach after them, careful not to control too much air but following at a safe distance. I didn't get far before the resistance increased. It was as if the distance was impacting how far I could reach, and I still had no idea where the dark elves were going or if *the* dark elf was there.

Taking a couple of steps forward, I gave myself more reach since more of the dark elves were ending up on the other side of the portal. I felt a hand on my arm.

*Careful, Aella. You don't want to get into a mental battle on the other side of a portal you don't yet know enough about. And if he feels you over there, he will try to latch on.*

Zephyr was right, but I sighed. It was helpful to know what lay beyond our world and what might come through to us, but we had to be careful.

I stopped and pulled back as soon as the last dark elves were sent home. Once again, it felt as if my mind traveled on the end of a thread through the portal, more time passing than I'd have liked as I wrestled with the strange sensation.

Finally, I was back in the portal room alone. By the time I got back, everyone was staring at me, the battle over.

"What were you doing?" Simon asked.

"Reaching through the portal with my mind as the dark elf does," I replied, not seeing the point of hiding it. "I wanted to know if it was possible."

"And was it?" he asked as Cherisse came marching over.

"Yes. But I need to practice my reach."

"Then do so and get the hell out of here," Cherisse replied. "I don't need you going rogue and upsetting the plans we've made."

"Upsetting your plans? You'd never have won that fight without me and my mythicals," I said, clenching my fists.

"You'd like to think that, wouldn't you? But all you've done is show them exactly what we have. While they're probing and trying to learn us, the longer it takes them to work out our full strength, the longer we have to prepare and find the elves on that side who can help us or come here for safety. You never think about anything but showing off and being the one to do everything."

I growled at the final accusation, but Zephyr projected calmness my way. As much as I hated to admit it, Cherisse had a point and my anger turned inward.

Thankfully, someone came up to Cherisse to let her know how many elves were injured, or worse, dead.

I gulped as I thought about how many couldn't be saved. Cherisse's strategy was coming at a price.

# CHAPTER ELEVEN

The dawn sun streamed into the room we'd been assigned as I tried to get more sleep. I was grateful to rest, but it hadn't been easy. I wasn't able to stop thinking about everything that had happened over the last twenty-four hours. Everything we'd learned and the conflict with Cherisse was buzzing around my head.

*It must be hard for her,* Zephyr said. *She's been in charge here for a long time, and she's got plans and schemes, and then Simon made you.*

*And I've upset a lot of her plans.*

We *have. They probably didn't expect the Henera to have four mythical creatures as well. She also probably didn't expect so many elves in the mountain to decide to subvert her authority to aid us. While some clearly don't appreciate our presence, others are warming to us.*

I sighed. It was true. There was no doubt about it. I was making Cherisse feel threatened, and I had no idea how to stop doing so.

For now, however, the best course of action was the

same. We needed to cooperate, help where we could, and learn what we could of the enemy. Especially if they were learning about us.

Slowly I drifted in and out of sleep, aware of Zephyr as he wrapped his tail around me and comforted me. I could feel Sen, Roth, and Nuri as well as they slept close by, their minds peaceful. I took comfort that we were together and one team. If nothing else, we were facing this dark elf as one.

There were still more questions about what he was capable of, however, and I didn't understand how his powers and abilities worked. But I was going to find out as soon as I could. If Cherisse didn't want me to help defend the portal unless I was summoned, then I needed to find other ways to aid in the fight.

I thought about Simon and what he must have done to make sure I was made. Had he done something similar? His experiments making me had been something he was passionate about, but had they been his way of making sure he helped when he didn't have another option from Cherisse?

It made me want to go see him and ask for more information again, but I also knew I needed to work out how to extend my abilities through the portal. I didn't like the air elf or working with him. I might have accepted him as an ally, but it would take me far longer to forgive him for Ascan.

When someone brought us breakfast a short while later, I was eager to get up. I noticed the bearer had a slight limp and looked exhausted as he came over to put the large platters of food on our table.

"Are you okay?" I asked, using air to take the weight off him.

"Just a small injury. There was another attack in the night. I got sloppy."

"No one let me know. I'd have helped."

The elf looked uncomfortable as I finished speaking.

"Let me guess, Cherisse made it very clear that I wasn't supposed to be told?"

"Sorry, Henera. I wanted to tell you, but when Cherisse decides something has to be a certain way..."

"It's okay," I replied, wanting to put him at ease. "As much as I want to help and make sure we repel the invaders, I know this needs to have someone calling the shots. We'll do what we can in other ways. Hopefully, we can stop some injuries from happening."

"And with any luck save some lives as well. We lost another five elves last night," he said as his shoulders slumped.

I gaped, not sure what to say, but aware any lives lost were too many, especially given that we had no idea how many were on the other side. We'd killed some of the dark elves, but it wasn't as many as we'd lost.

*I don't think I can do nothing*, I told Zephyr, not sure what else to say.

*We won't do nothing. But if we piss off Cherisse, she'll kick us out of the mountain.*

It was a good point.

"I'll do what I can," I said aloud to the elf. "Can you let me know when there is an attack anyway? I might be able to help in ways that don't make Cherisse angry."

The elf hesitated, frowning and shifting his weight around.

"Okay," he said a moment later. "But please be careful what you do. If she knew I was telling you..."

"I'll be careful. I don't want to get you in trouble."

"It's a good thing Simon likes you and you're the Henera," he added with a grin before hurrying away.

I smiled, beginning to feel better again. Cherisse might be trying to block my progress, but she wasn't going to stop me from finding ways to help, especially if people were dying.

Zephyr morphed into his human form and we ate quickly, grateful that the elf had brought us large platters of food. He wrapped an arm around me as we ate, letting me feel the warmth of his body. I could also feel the emotions under the surface. Finding out his mother had given his egg to the Amcika elves was weighing on his mind as much as the other information was weighing on mine.

After we'd eaten, I stuffed some fruit into a pocket, then we made our way to the portal site. I wanted to see what I could do while my abilities were recharged.

There were a few elves nearby, and they looked exhausted, though several of them smiled when they saw me. I returned the gesture but didn't wait for anyone to stop me or question what I was doing.

Getting close to the portal, I found the best place to stand so if an attack started, I wasn't going to be bumped into or spotted the second dark elves appeared. The closest place I could think of was behind the portal and looking up toward it. I waited for the others to spread out around me, the four mythicals mostly facing the portal and any possible threats as an extra line of defense.

If anything could make me feel as if I was part of a team and valued by my mythicals, this was it. They were protecting me without me asking, and I was doing what I could to get us some answers.

I could feel many eyes on me as I focused my mind on the air and then reached around to the front of the portal. While I trusted the mythicals to let me know what was going on here, I closed my eyes to concentrate more easily and moved my mind through the air and into the portal. It resisted entry at first, but then, as it had the first time I'd tried, my mind was grabbed and whisked away.

Although it still felt sudden and almost violent, it wasn't as unexpected and I relaxed into the process, feeling around while I was in the portal. It was a strange sensation, but there was a fast-moving tube, like being on a slide and having to keep going.

The sensation was less firm now and then, but I was unable to work out why. Eventually, I was spat out on the other side, and my mind reached more of the strange air element that was so marked by use and control from the dark elf and those with him. Although it was marked, I had begun working out the pattern it had.

I didn't try to connect very much, not wanting to make it too obvious my mind was there, but I did connect to and reach out more. I wanted to know how easy it was to maintain a connection while I was rested and had plenty of capacity. How close was I to the level of power the dark elf had? Did I need practice? Had he simply been better rested than me?

The dark elf's reach was still greater than mine. I was close to the portal and still feeling as if I was a long way off being able to reach out as far as I'd like on the other side. Especially given how far he had reached out at the last attack on the Texas portal. It had been a challenge for me to push him back as well, the elements feeling the weight of his mark long after his mind had entered the portal again.

*Cherisse is here*, Zephyr said a moment later. *I think she wants to know what you're doing.*

*Does it look like she's going to stop me?* I replied, worried we were about to have a disagreement while my mind was deep in the portal and I could be in danger.

*I won't let her, even if she tries.* A determined wave came off Zephyr, and I was comforted by his ability to defend me. Everything I could do with the elements, he could also. That meant Cherisse alone couldn't do anything. Of course, she wasn't alone, and we needed to keep her happy, but Zephyr kept a far cooler head than I did. He was far better suited to the task of keeping the cult head from lashing out at us in anger.

Although I could vaguely hear talking in the background and a woman's voice conversing with Zephyr, I focused again on the other side of the portal and what I could feel.

There were several guards around the portal, each trying to hide and each one holding onto the earth or air nearest them. I tried to feel along without alerting them, but I was pretty sure one of them picked up on my mind as I pushed deeper and then tried to avoid my contact.

They shifted, and their connection strengthened. I

almost pulled back, retreating, but instead, I opted to keep perfectly still, my mind touching the elements exactly as I had been. I then, very slowly, released them all, making sure my grip matched the marker on the element as best as I could.

Fear filled me, certain I would be noticed and the elf would either attack me mentally or push me back, but as I retreated, the elf relaxed, settling into a sitting position behind a short wall or fortification.

I continued to explore for the next few minutes, probing farther out, but I found my limit again. I managed to determine that there were at least six elves around the portal guarding it and then more in rooms nearby that felt like barracks. I couldn't detect exactly how many there were there, but I did know they appeared to be resting.

It was good news. If everyone was sleeping, it meant there wasn't going to be another attack yet. It also made it easier for me to push out farther and feel around for possible others. Of course, I soon found myself near the end of my reach. I had explored farther than before and I moved outward in several directions, but there was no sign of the dark elf, and I didn't know where he might be.

Exasperated, I pushed harder. He had to be around here somewhere. No matter how hard I tried, however, I couldn't get any deeper, and I was more aware of the voices talking nearby. Frustrated and not having learned much, I pulled back and let my mind make the journey back through the portal.

It felt as if it took ages, but I was sure it hadn't. Cherisse was irate at Zephyr and possibly Roth as well. I couldn't be sure when my mind returned to this side of the portal what had been said in my absence, but it must have been serious. With Cherisse glaring at me, it was clear Zephyr had done all he could.

"You didn't have permission to be here or interfere," she said, the anger in her voice obvious.

"You know, you once told me that if the evil still lurked on the other side of this portal, you'd be proud to wade into battle beside the Henera," I replied.

"That was before you betrayed us and lied. You have no honor and no understanding of what it is to truly be an elf. And you'll get away from the portal I control."

I sighed, trying not to let my anger get the better of me. After taking a deep breath, I put myself in Cherisse's shoes.

"You're right that I lied to you. You'd kidnapped me and were pushing me to do something that seemed incredibly unsafe and not our decision to make. But whether we disagree on that or not, the evil lurks on the other side of the portal as we feared. It doesn't matter which one of us is right or wrong, or whether we like each other, even. If we don't work together, *he* will win, and neither of us can afford that. So...why don't we both come away from the portal and find a way to do this?"

I thought Cherisse was going to refuse, her arms folding across her chest as she continued to glare. But eventually, she relaxed.

"I'm learning as I take my mind through the portal. It could help you and the other elves here. Let me tell you what I felt on the other side."

"Intel would be useful," she acknowledged, calming. Without another word, she stood to the side to make way for me to walk beside her.

With my mythicals following, Cherisse and I headed away from the portal. Every eye was on us, many of them wider than usual. I had won a victory, but I knew it wasn't likely to become a friendship any time soon.

Within minutes, we were sitting in what looked like a command room, rosters of names on the walls and a makeshift miniature cave and portal structure on a table.

I told her everything I'd learned from trips through the portal with my mind and described the difficulty of range and how it was much harder to control the elements on that side than it was here. The latter didn't seem to surprise her, but she got up and went over to a small book-shelf. She picked up a book and handed it to me.

"This might help. But that's the last time you approach the portal without notifying me first. I want to make sure I'm there and I know what you're doing on the other side. If you trigger an attack and I've not approved of what you're doing, I'm going to have you expelled from this mountain."

"I shouldn't need to ask your permission to do what needs to be done," I snapped back without thinking.

"And this is my mountain. You might be the Henera, but you answer to me. You were always supposed to answer to me."

I growled, but a wave of calm came from Zephyr, and he touched my arm.

"We should go get some rest," he said aloud so Cherisse would also get the warning.

Before I could argue with him and also tell Cherisse what I thought of her arrogance, an elf rushed in.

"Attack," he shouted.

Cherisse sprinted to the door.

"Stay here or go rest, but do not approach the portal," she snapped at me before I could respond or move.

*We should respect that,* Zephyr said.

I sighed and deflated. No part of me wanted to stay out of the situation, but there wasn't much I could do to change it right now. Being chucked out of the mountain would make it harder to help.

# CHAPTER TWELVE

As I ate and tried not to worry, I listened to the sounds of the battle raging down the corridor. Zephyr and I had eventually agreed that the five of us should wait down the hallway from the portal. A reserve in case we were needed.

Cherisse had noticed us as she'd helped Simon limp back our way, his nose bleeding and his body tired, but she'd simply helped the older elf down to sit near us and then hurried back to the battle. I grabbed a rag from the makeshift first aid station that was set up nearby and wiped his nose with it before sticking a bread roll in his hands.

He gave me an appreciative smile before taking a bite.

While there wasn't a lot else I could do, I decided to be a medic, and I kept the food coming for any of the elves who came our way drained, injured, or otherwise unable to fight. It earned me frowns when I requested more bread and fruit from the person who had brought the food up to the portal floor, but Simon added his weight to my request, and the elf ran off to do my bidding.

I was bandaging a sprained ankle under directions from an elf beside me who was dressing another wound when an elf with tears streaming down her face floated the limp, robe-covered form of an elf past us. I gulped, knowing that it could only mean another dead elf.

When this happened for the sixth time, I got up, wanting to go to the portal and join the fight. Zephyr came to my side, wishing to do the same, but Simon called my name.

"You'll save a life or two now, Henera, but you'll get yourself kicked out of the mountain and then more will die. Cherisse will either be right about this tactic, or she'll come to her senses soon. The more you push her, the more she'll dig her heels in. Do what you can as you are now."

"This isn't enough," I replied through gritted teeth.

"Then work with me. I could do with your abilities."

I frowned, not sure I wanted to work with someone who had killed a friend of mine, but I couldn't deny that I was intrigued by his proposal. What could he mean about me being able to help him? The dark elf was on the other side of the portal, attacking. What could he do from this side?

"When this fight is over and we've had a chance to rest, come down to my lab," Simon continued, slowly getting to his feet. "Give me a chance to explain. I heard what you said to Cherisse earlier about not having to like each other. Well, you don't have to like me either, and I wouldn't blame you for hating me. I know what I've done and how distasteful it is to the noblest of us, but we want the same thing. To defeat that dark elf and keep this world safe. I'll work with you if you'll work with me. I'll listen to your suggestions."

Every part of me wanted to refuse, but it was an offer I couldn't refuse, especially after the way I'd talked to Cherisse.

"I have one condition."

"Name it."

"No one else dies by your hands or anyone you control. And not because we need them for this fight, because lives matter, and they should never be thrown away. There's always another way."

"While I might disagree on that last part, I consider your help of more value than you'd understand. I'll do as you ask."

I gave Simon a curt nod and then got out of the way so he could go and rest.

Although I wasn't sure how he could walk away from an unfinished battle, I saw the exhausted look that flashed across his face when he realized the elevator was offline. It was brief, but he was far more drained than any elf I'd seen in a long time. He needed to rest and was no good to anyone to continue fighting.

I turned my attention back to the medic beside me as another two injured elves came toward us and then collapsed. Blood was pouring out of the wound on one. I knelt beside them, and as the medic had shown me, I reached into the elf's body with my mind and took control of the blood near the wound. Very gently, I stopped it from flowing, helping it clot and solidify the area around the wound so the elf didn't bleed out.

Although I was very unsure of what I was doing, it

worked, and the elf relaxed as the medic quickly stabilized the other elf and then came to help me. I let them take over and backed off. I'd done what was needed without thinking about it. I looked down at the exhausted, pale elf who was breathing heavily through pain.

*You probably saved his life*, Zephyr said. *The medic wouldn't have been able to get to him in time.*

Zephyr was right, but I still felt as if this could have been spared were I in the fight. Were we in the fight. My mythicals and I had trained for so long for things like this. We could make a difference in a better way.

As suddenly as the attack had begun, however, it ended. The mountain was silent, the deafening quiet continuing until an injured person groaned as the medic set their broken bone in place.

This broke the dam since someone else coughed, and the noise slowly filled in again. I took a couple of steps toward the portal, terrified that it hadn't ended in our favor. I didn't get any farther before Cherisse appeared, striding toward me as her cloak and dress billowed out behind her. She looked as grim as ever.

"Get some rest," she said to me as she passed. "It's over, and we won. You don't have to hang around and try not to get in the way."

It was a gentler encouragement to leave than normal, but it was still that. Although I wanted to say so much, Simon had possibly given me another way, and I was curious enough about what that was that I didn't argue and instead led my mythicals away.

While we waited for Simon to rest, there wasn't much we could do, so we went back to our room. We watched the sun move across the sky, mostly obscured by light clouds but sometimes coming out to brighten the side of the mountain. I briefly wondered where Minsheng and the others were and what they would be doing and thinking.

I decided to message them and let them know more about what was happening. I'd let them know I was in the mountain and that the dark elf was as active as we'd feared, but I hadn't said much more. Although it felt as if a lot had happened, I hadn't been in the mountain long. I was sure Minsheng would appreciate an update, however.

Finally, as the sun began setting, I decided that I'd let Simon rest for long enough. I wasn't sure he'd be in his laboratory, but it would give me a chance to snoop around if he wasn't. Zephyr had offered to keep watch while I ransacked the lab, but I was pretty sure we had all the information available on how our lives began.

I was grateful to find the elevator working again, but it still made me feel more claustrophobic than normal, and I was grateful to get out of it when we reached our destination. I then made my way along to the room I'd found Simon in a day or so before.

Despite how little time had passed since the battle and Simon having decided to rest, I found the elf in the lab looking over a test with test tubes, fire, and other items I didn't recognize.

As soon as he saw me he smiled.

"Ah, Henera, come in, come in. I must confess that I wasn't sure that I was going to see you this evening. I had begun to suspect that you had changed your mind about my offer."

"I haven't yet, but I reserve the right to hear what you have to say before I commit either way."

"I'd expect nothing else. It's not easy to begin trusting someone you've not met until recently, especially given the history and how we've come to be working together."

"Yeah... I generally think people prefer being asked to visit their parental home," I replied. "And to know that's what it is."

Simon gave me a tiny nod, the only acknowledgment he'd ever made that he hadn't given me a great start in life and that I had felt abandoned.

I tried not to freak out at this point, wanting to be in another place that wasn't with him and to process more of what I'd learned. Zephyr sent a calming balm of emotions to me in a wave.

Knowing that he was trying to help, I let it wash through me and held on to how it felt.

"Okay," I said. "Tell me your idea, and maybe we'll make it work."

"It's fairly simple," Simon replied, beckoning me over to the nearest workbench. It was one I'd not paid much attention to because the majority of it had been obscured by the experiment he was conducting and then him, but I gave it my attention now.

It had a couple of books open to one side, the leather-bound tomes looking as if they'd come from the mountain's library. To the side of it was a journal and a pen, no doubt Simon's notes.

But the bit that drew my attention was the diagram of the inside of an elf's mind. It was similar enough to a human's that at first glance, you couldn't see that much of a difference. I noticed it was different, however. There were some highlighted regions and the symbol of the different elements drawn in them.

"Does that show that a different part of the mind controls different elements?" I asked.

"Yes. It seems to be so. And technology has made that possible to know only recently. But it's not been tested very extensively. Of course, I've looked at how a brain lights up when I'm getting elves to control a single element. But I have no idea what happens when an elf controls more than one."

"So, you want to study my brain?"

"Yes, pretty much."

"How is this supposed to help?"

"Because the only two elves who can control everything are you and him. If I can work out how, maybe I can either unlock more or figure out how to block him."

I frowned at the thought of the last part. If it could be used against him, in theory, it could also be used against me.

"I know what you fear," he said as if he could read my mind. "And I can't entirely put that fear to rest. You'll have to decide if you trust me or not. But I made you. I wanted the Henera to come to this planet so badly I devoted decades to the process. And then I gave you up so you'd grow in the environment you needed. Away from someone like Cherisse who would have taught you to be nothing but a killing machine."

"Yet you killed someone to get me to chase you to the portal and open it for you."

"I did, which proves my point. When you live in this

environment for a long time, you begin to feel as if anything is okay as long as it furthers that goal. I know it won't change anything but, for what it's worth, I regret taking the young elf's life. Necessary or not, it has haunted me every day since."

"And yet you dragged me back here." I was being petty now, wanting to argue with him. He'd already explained enough.

"I did, once I knew you had become the Henera you ought to be. You need compassion. You need to have family around you. Functional examples of relationships. People worth saving. You couldn't get any of that here, but we still need you."

"Or you'd have created just another dark elf with a lust for power."

"Yes. And there was a chance that I was doing that anyway. That living among humanity would have made you exactly like the weaknesses of the species. But they have a capacity to love, forgive, and bond in ways that elves struggle to understand. You needed that variety."

I gulped as tears threatened to fall. I was pretty sure he was telling the truth, but even if he wasn't, I had to trust this elf in front of me. If I was going to be different from the dark elf and become someone worth following into battle, I had to model good behavior. I had to care and trust and choose to open myself up to pain and criticism. I had to be better than so many others.

"Okay," I said, eventually. "I'll help you. But I want to understand along the way, and we're doing this together. For the greater good. If this saves even one life, I'll consider it worth it, but if you do use this against me, know that either I or my mythicals will find a way to make you pay for it. I'm going to defeat the dark elf. If you hinder me, I'll consider you to be his ally and just as bad."

"Noted. I would expect nothing less. And if nothing else, you've picked up on the human capacity to make it very clear who is in charge."

I heard Zephyr chuckle at the subtle dig of being so forthright.

*I'm not sure I find that funny,* I thought to Zephyr.

*Oh, it's not funny for the reasons Simon thinks it is. It's rude to suggest that you're somehow being bossy. You're not, and if you were male, no one would think twice about the things you've said.*

*So what made you chuckle?*

*That Simon feels threatened by you and is finally being polite. He wasn't, to begin with, but I think he's more aware of what you're capable of now. Your confidence and ability are intimidating to him. But it's entirely him showing his hand.*

I thought about Zephyr's words as Simon ushered me over to a chair he wanted me to get into. It was black leather and like a dentist's chair. The kind that can be tilted and reclined and raised. I almost didn't get into it, remembering how scary the chair had been at my dentist's. Dentists could be terrifying.

I sat down, however, and focused again. Although I didn't entirely understand everything Zephyr was trying to say to me, I appreciated that he wasn't laughing at me but thought there was nothing wrong with my confidence.

As soon as I was in position, Simon attached a bunch of sticky pads with wires coming out of them onto my forehead and around my head.

"Right," he said. "We need to do one element at a time. And just one. No using the second, third, or fourth. Not even a little."

"Start with air then," I replied, knowing I used it the most instinctively and would struggle to let it go entirely for him to be able to get a clear reading on the other three.

Simon didn't seem to care where I began but told me to relax, and I began doing things with the air as he suggested for me to test myself. At first, he just wanted me to play, but with each instruction, he got me to push myself more. As he did, my brain lit up on the screen we were studying.

It was cool but also strange to see the image of my brain change based on what I was doing. I tested it myself over the next little while, noticing when I pushed myself that it grew brighter.

Once Simon was satisfied with the air element, we moved on to the other three. As I suspected, I found it harder to isolate my use of them, the desire to keep connected with the air more present than with the other elements. I did notice that my control of the earth was also occasionally there, and it made me realize I was beginning to feel the ground beneath my feet and the plants nearby on automatic.

I still wasn't sure how it would help us fight the dark elf, but it was fascinating, and it gave me some insight into how my powers had developed. I was growing stronger, and I was learning to use my abilities instinctively. It would make me harder to defeat.

# CHAPTER THIRTEEN

As the sun came up on another day, I rolled over and ignored it. I'd worked late with Simon in the lab, trying to understand everything he talked about and everything he knew of the brain. He'd called on another elf who had been a scientist and a gnome I didn't recognize to aid him in working out what could be done.

At midnight I had excused myself, hungry and drained from pushing my abilities while being monitored. It had been a tiring day. I was glad I'd done it, but it could still come to nothing, and I would still have to fight the dark elf.

There had been talk of using drugs to block parts of the brain, but of course, there was no way to know the dark elf's mind lit up the way mine did. And there was no way to know that the elven body wouldn't ignore drugs that had been designed and trialed on humans.

The three scientists had then talked of many things I didn't understand, despite my best efforts to do so. In the end, I'd given up and gone to sleep. I'd also been aware that as much as I had been aided by the stint with Simon, that my mythicals were bored and had been sitting around a long time.

It wasn't ideal for any of us to be in the mountain with little to do, but I cared about them and what they could do as well.

We'd used up more power playing around in the room we'd been allocated, and then we'd gotten some sleep. Now, however, I didn't want to be awake. As the room got brighter, I was aware I wasn't likely to have a choice, however. Nuri's mind became more alert, and the bird untucked his head from beneath his wing.

When Zephyr also stirred beside me, it was too late. We were awake, and once our minds kicked in and fed each other subtle emotional tells and hints of thoughts, we were all likely to wake up.

Breakfast arrived and killed my objections to getting up. I was always so hungry that it was one of my favorite meals. The others had a hearty appetite as well.

We were finishing up when Cherisse appeared.

"I understand you were working with Simon last night," she said as she strode into my room, no other introduction to the conversation and no request to enter a space supposed to be mine for a while.

I frowned but nodded, wondering where she was going with this.

"Simon has an interesting talent and dedication to advancing our goals. I appreciate that you're willing to work with him. I want to make it very clear that you still report to me while you're in this mountain, however."

"Got it," I replied, hoping this wasn't going to go somewhere that made me have to decide between keeping my word to her and breaking my sense of morality.

"Good. Because Simon sometimes gets strange ideas, and he doesn't always take the time to explain everything."

I frowned without thinking, feeling as if I'd had the opposite problem. Simon had explained so much and in so much detail that my head had spun. There was something about his manner that made me feel as if Cherisse was likely to be the difficult one in this equation, but I also knew Simon could be showing me favoritism the others didn't get the luxury of. After all, he had created me.

"Is that the only reason you came to see me?" I asked when Cherisse still lingered. "Can I possibly help with anything else?"

She narrowed her eyes, and I thought she was going to open her mouth and say something. Nothing came out, however. She turned to go and leave me again.

"How is the defense going?" I asked. "Would it help for me to push through the portal and explore again today?"

Cherisse stopped again and turned to half face me before she stared off into the distance.

"The defense is...mixed. I can't afford to lose many more good elves or see them injured, but it helps my cause while we beat the dark elf's forces and make him think he needs to increase his attack. And I know there are elves out there to find."

"Does he always hold this portal?" I asked.

"You're the only one with any knowledge of the other side. The brave elves I have sent through have not returned. So you tell me. Does he always hold this portal?"

I exhaled, hearing the frustration in her voice. Although

it wasn't much of an acknowledgment of what I was doing, I appreciated the candor I was being given, even if it came with aggression.

"It would appear so. I think so. Both of the previous times I reached through, it felt as if his presence had been there recently, but I didn't feel him there directly."

"He hasn't assaulted us after each attack the last few times either. It's as if he's not there at the moment."

Cherisse's words made me think. There was a lot I'd not told her or anyone else in the mountain about what had happened at the other portal site. I'd connected with the dark elf more times than I wanted to talk about. Each time I'd grown better at resisting him but he was also learning more about me.

While I didn't think there was anything I could have done about the latter, not when I was also learning a lot, I wondered if maybe I could find a way to learn more about him by pooling our knowledge. Could we give ourselves an advantage?

*It's worth a try at this point. Everyone knowing as much as they can increases our chances of survival*, Zephyr pointed out.

I wasn't going to argue with the logic, knowing how many times more information had helped us defeat something. With that in mind, I told Cherisse everything about the few encounters I'd had with the dark elf, including what he had done and was doing at the other portal site.

"Thank you," Cherisse said when I was done, sitting at the small dining table I had and snacking on fruit with me. "That makes it clearer that he intends to not only break through here but elsewhere as well."

"It would seem so. But the Texas portal still has its pillars. There's no one trying to break those."

"Then let us hope it remains so. Although..."

"What?" I asked as Cherisse's voice trailed off.

"There are elves who are sympathetic to our cause on the other side somewhere, I'm sure. Or enslaved elves we could rescue if nothing else. Your story of connecting at least once to a very different elf confirms that."

"It does, but I don't think we can defend two portal sites right now."

"We're defending this one successfully."

"Are you?" I asked, quick to reply. "You're losing lives every time, and that's without the dark elf applying pressure the last few times."

This time Cherisse frowned. I'd hit a nerve, but it was something that needed pointing out to her. She'd made it clear that she was arrogant enough to keep throwing lives away in the past. If I could maybe save a few, it was worth a try. After all, she only had so many elves in the mountain. And the humans weren't doing anything to help yet.

Instead of responding in any way, however, she got to her feet.

"How rested are you feeling?" she asked when she was partway to the door.

"Well enough. I was hoping to try feeling through the portal again. Assuming you have no objection?"

"No. I think it would be good to find out more about what this dark elf is up to. We can't defend like this forever. Not without learning more."

I felt as if the two of us might finally be understanding each other as I grabbed my jacket and followed her out of the room. Given that the mythicals were coming with me, I considered something more daring. Going through the portal, though that was a far bigger risk.

*If he's not there and we can attack the elves nearest without going through, we might be able to get to the other side, even if briefly,* Zephyr pointed out.

I was about to tell him that was a bad idea when I realized he was right. My mind and reach could do a lot on the other side. With Zephyr's help, it might be possible to make sure that Kirdash wasn't there and then take out anyone watching the portal so we could slip through and explore farther on the other side.

Of course, I had no intention of pointing this out to Cherisse. There was no way she'd necessarily approve of such a risk, but she wanted answers, and we'd attempt to attack the elves on the other side and go through if we were sure that we could do so fairly safely.

No part of me wanted to go through and then be captured or worse. It was dangerous to even consider it.

*We have to try something. At the moment, he's walking all over us and killing elves in the mountain,* Zephyr pointed out. *This place won't hold forever, even with our help.*

*Sen go through portal,* she added, looking up at me from her perch in my jacket.

*If one of us goes, we'll all go. I'm not having us split between worlds,* I replied, knowing Zephyr wouldn't let me go without him.

*That might be more dangerous for Roth, Nuri, and Sen,* Zephyr told me, and I was pretty sure he kept the words from the others as well.

*But not you?* I asked, knowing he was thinking about the

way the dark elf was supposed to be able to do something to the bonds with mythicals.

*I think I can help fight it.*

*Nuri can do so as well. He's been helping me fight on behalf of all of you.*

*Good point.* Zephyr let out a sigh, and his guard came down with it. I could feel the worry that bubbled under the surface.

*We don't have to try to go through if you're this bothered by it. I thought you had suggested it because it was what you wanted?*

*It's going to be needed. And at some point, I think we'll have to face him over there. Another planet where the elements are marked is a big thing to be facing, though.*

*And we'll face it together like everything else.*

*Together.*

*All five of us.*

*Yes. All of us.* Zephyr gave me a brief nod and I focused on where I was going again.

I noticed Cherisse glancing between Zephyr and me and was pretty sure she'd picked up on the two of us having a mental conversation. If she was curious, she didn't voice it.

The elevator ride to the portal felt like it took forever though it was only a few floors. I was tense and beginning to worry about what might lie in wait for us. I had a good imagination and knew there was a chance that the dark elf was hoping we'd try exactly this. There was a possibility that the dark elf was just beyond the edge of my range, waiting for us.

*If he is, we can retreat through the portal pretty swiftly.*

*We're not going far from it on the other side. Not on this trip through.*

*Hopefully, not on any trip through*, I replied, appreciating Zephyr.

After we finished reassuring each other, I walked up to the portal. I could feel everyone looking at me, but they seemed more relaxed and openly curious, given Cherisse was aware of everything this time. Thankfully, she hung back near the edge of the natural cavern and left us to do the experimenting without her.

Part of me wanted to demand that she take the risk along with us. After all, she'd opened the portal, but it was petty of me. It also made sense not to use up her energy in case the dark elf did send in another wave of attackers before we'd had a chance to rest. I couldn't expend my energy and then leave the mountain without enough strong elves to defend it.

With this as my last thought, I stepped forward and concentrated. My mythicals were standing close by me. Sen was on one shoulder and Nuri on the other. Roth and Zephyr were on either side of me, ready to go through the portal with me as soon as I gave the signal.

Although Zephyr could also have projected his mind along with mine, he was hanging back as well, no sense in both of us struggling to have enough energy later.

I slipped my mind into the portal again, reaching for the elements on the other side of it. Once again, there was a strange jarring sensation, and I had to grit my teeth at how uncomfortable it was. Hoping that it wasn't trans-lating too powerfully to my mythicals, I held on and waited until I was spat out at the other end.

Although I had no idea how it worked to transport only my elemental reach across the dimensions or space or whatever was between our worlds, I was grateful it did as I felt the air on the other side and the strange sensation lessened.

I took several deep, slow breaths as I calmed myself well enough to think and reach out properly. I had to get this right. Although I could feel the control of other elves, I slipped around it, going up and over and around, trying not to trigger awareness of my presence.

As before, no one moved on the other side of the portal, but I quickly identified several air and earth elementals nearby, watching the portal and waiting. I tried to work out how they could or would alert the rest of the elves if there was an attack next, feeling for an alarm or trigger.

There didn't seem to be anything, which made me more worried. There had to be some way that they communicated.

*They might do so mentally. Like we do*, Zephyr said.

I frowned. If that was true, there wasn't going to be a way for us to take them out and not alert the rest of the elves there. I moved outward from them, trying to work out where the rest were and what might be happening. If they were asleep as they had been the time before, I might stand a chance.

Of course, the last time I'd felt through the portal, it hadn't been long after an attack, and they'd had good reason to be resting. This time it was longer since the last altercation. I had no idea what to expect.

Reaching out toward the edge of my limits, I found the barrack-style room again. It was surprisingly full of sleeping elves, all of them still and quiet. I kept my presence moving gently along, barely touching the edge of the elements before I moved on, but they didn't seem to be particularly controlled by anyone, although the marked feeling was still very much there.

I moved around the edge of my limit entirely, taking my time while trying not to wear myself out too much. By the time I was done, I had found nothing new. The only elves awake were the few watching the portal. There was no sign of the dark elf.

Now I had to decide what I did about it.

*Knock them out and let's go through*, Zephyr said.

I hesitated a moment before deciding to do so. I'd make an air box around their heads. They'd pass out, and no one would be any the wiser.

Grinning, I formed the boxes. It was time to see what was on the other side of the portal.

# CHAPTER FOURTEEN

It only took seconds to get the boxes formed, and then the last sections went into place. I had made them as small as I could get away with, wanting the oxygen to run out quickly enough that it did so at roughly the same time for all of the guards. It wasn't entirely precise, but it was the best I could do while so far away.

I let the others know to be prepared to step through the portal and then waited. As soon as they were out cold, we were going through.

Before long they began to wobble, the air running low enough that they went lightheaded. I made sure their little box of air followed them as they slipped down to the ground, holding onto the air for long enough that they wouldn't wake up again right away. I was worried about killing them, but I had to make sure that they didn't wake up while we were in the portal.

As the last one passed out, I let my mythicals know. I took a step toward the portal, but the moment I did, another elf appeared on the edge of the area I was monitoring. And then another, and another.

The elves had woken up, and they were coming to the portal. I stayed where I was. The elves were coming in formation, marching as if ready for battle and heading straight for the portal. I wasn't sure if I'd triggered them or not, but it didn't take them long to notice the downed elves and the commotion was instant.

*Pull back,* Zephyr said. *You need to get your mind back on this side so we can move you back and away from the portal.*

I almost panicked, but Zephyr was right. I quickly pulled my mind back, bumping into the control of several elves as they reached into the air to work out what was happening. No doubt I'd made them aware of me, but it was more important to be fast right now.

*Warn Cherisse that an attack is incoming,* I replied to my mythicals as more elves poured into the square around the portal on the other side. They were sending far more this time.

It felt like it took ages for my mind to come back through the portal. I could hear Cherisse yelling orders, and I could feel Zephyr's arm around my waist.

Nuri, Seth, and Roth had pulled away from the portal, but Zephyr wouldn't leave me, knowing I would be vulnerable at first.

Although I appreciated the care he was showing toward me, it also made me worry that he was putting himself in danger unnecessarily, and I wanted him to be safe as well.

I could withstand a few dark elves, especially if he and many other elves were standing ready. And I'd bought the mountain some warning this time. There were elves in place ready to defend.

That said, I noticed Cherisse was holding some back still, not seeming to understand that this attack was going to be far worse than the previous ones,

*More elves are coming to wait down the corridor*, Zephyr reassured me, his mind still connected with mine despite me floating in a portal more than being present in my body. It was a strange feeling of being in two places at once, and I didn't like it.

I sighed with relief as my mind came back into the cavern and my eyes came back into alignment. No sooner had I begun to turn my head toward Zephyr than he pulled me toward him, turning me and tugging me away from the portal.

Sen and Nuri were sitting on Roth's back near the corridor and Simon, and I noticed they weren't being ushered back any farther.

"What did you do?" Cherisse asked as I took the first few steps away.

"I don't think it was anything I did," I replied, although there was a part of me that wasn't sure.

"Zephyr said you were attacking the portal guards when some dark elves appeared."

"I wasn't attacking in any way they'd have detected. The army appeared far too soon for me to have caused it. I swear."

She didn't look convinced, but I could see her eyes get wider as she heard me say army.

"How many?" she asked.

"At least a hundred. Probably more."

"That's over double the previous maximum."

"We're going to need as many defenders as possible," I said, hoping she understood what was coming.

"We can't fit that many in here, but we won't let them through. I think you should probably stick around this time."

It was the first time she'd conceded to needing my help, and I was grateful for the opportunity. If this was going to be the reason, I was able to cope with it. No part of me wanted to be in yet another life or death battle, but I couldn't sit around and do nothing.

"Head down the corridor with the others," Cherisse said a moment later, looking at the portal.

I opened my mouth to protest at that not being what I'd thought, but Zephyr's grip around my waist tightened, and he pulled me farther away.

*Let it go. She'll realize how much she needs us soon enough.* Zephyr's words came out calm, but I could feel the anger he was trying not to project. I wasn't the only one who thought this was wrong.

Once I reached Roth, Nuri, and Sen flew to my shoulders. Then the five of us made our way from the portal cavern and into the elf-made hallway beyond it.

There were a fair few elves out there as well, but it wasn't going to be enough. Even if I defeated half of the elves on the way, given the size of the incoming army, this many elves were going to be overrun.

Before I was somewhere we could rest and wait, I heard the sounds of battle. From here I couldn't see what was going on, but I noticed the elf appear who had administered first aid during the last fight I'd been present for. I gave her a nod and moved to help her set up a small, temporary workstation, not knowing what else I could do yet.

It was hard to be doing something so simple when a battle raged. Several times when I heard yells or Cherisse calling for the next wave, I had to fight the urge to get up and go to help. I soon had patients to help keep alive, however, since I was now used to stopping blood pouring out of bodies and helping the medics patch them and heal them.

I was grateful that the elven bodies were faster at healing than a normal human and responded to the treatments being given them. But when the first dead body came past, borne by an air elf, I couldn't take it any longer.

I got to my feet again, the injured elf I was helping no longer bleeding from a gash to his head, and looked for Zephyr. He was on his feet as well, frowning and looking toward the cavern.

We were striding that way, Roth with us as we bypassed several sets of nervous, waiting fighters and grew closer to the battle. Before we could get there, however, Simon came running toward us.

"Fall back," I heard Cherisse yell, and several elves did that. Simon stopped beside me and turned.

"Help me hold the line to get everyone out?" he asked.

Although he'd not needed to and I was preparing to do so, I nodded and grabbed more of the air above the heads of the elves, moving it around them and giving them a boost as they ran past me. The second I saw a dark elf, I blasted them off their feet and sent them reeling back.

There was still no sign of Cherisse, however. Nor some

of the other powerful elves who reported to her. It made Simon's frown deepen, and I worried that something had happened to her.

I took several steps forward as the number of dark elves grew before me, many of them beginning to recover from being blasted off their feet. Zephyr took control of the mountain rock and shook it under their feet or trapped them in its crushing embrace, but I focused on the air and used it to push the elves back as I continued to take steps forward.

I put up a full barrier across the entire corridor. It wasn't ideal to work on something so large when our people were on the other side of it, but I could feel the mounting attacks. They weren't going to go away any time soon, and I wasn't able to steady myself against everything.

Sen started hurling little ice pellets and using her small dart gun to put anyone who came close out cold. Nuri also leaped from my shoulder, turning into a fireball in the air as he flew closer. This was more of a distraction than anything, but I was grateful for it nonetheless.

I kept up the assault, slowly moving forward as Simon came too, sticking close to my side. He continued to feed the barrier as well, making the line of air colder as he'd inadvertently taught me to do the last time we were together.

Finally, Cherisse came running around the corner, a whirl of water around her as she moved, and one air elf carrying another dead elf, but there were at least twenty dark elves between her and us now. I saw the fear on her face, but it was momentary as she blasted the nearest enemies in her way off their feet.

I joined her attempts and wrapped her group in another barrier as Simon instinctively took up the act of protecting him and me. It wasn't ideal, but it allowed the elves with Cherisse to help her blast a path out.

By the time she reached me, there were so many dark elves focused on me and challenging the barrier I was creating that I was struggling.

*We need to fall back as well,* Zephyr said. *Get somewhere we can defend in a more open space and hit these elves harder.*

"Do you have a plan?" I asked Cherisse as she finally reached us and Simon dropped the barrier to give me a way to bring the others in. I wrapped the one I'd been holding around us as I fell in beside Cherisse and retreated with her, facing the enemy.

"Get to the stairwell," she replied, not entirely answering my question, but she didn't look at me either, ushering the other elves ahead of us.

While others helped the wounded move and the rest of the elves were obeying Cherisse, I held the same position longer, my head hurting under the direct challenge of what felt like tens of elves.

Zephyr had to put out fires, fight for control of the earth, and help people move, but my barrier held for now, and the elves retreated behind me.

Sen hopped up on my shoulder again and used what she could see to project to me everything that was happening with the elves so I could concentrate on the barrier. With Zephyr's arm to help guide me as well, I walked slowly backward, feeling my energy drain and my body shake with adrenaline and fear. I'd never held this many elves back before.

And more were appearing with every minute that passed.

By the time I reached the stairwell, the elves had gone down it. I briefly glanced at the elevator shaft on the other side of the hallway and noticed it was dark and flickering, the doors pried open, and no shiny metal box in sight.

"It's broken. Shattered into a thousand pieces at the bottom," Cherisse explained, seeing where I was looking. "The air elves could fly down that way if they truly wanted to, but they'll meet several powerful air elves waiting way up from the bottom and a dead-end at the very last section.

I nodded, hoping it was enough. Technically there was nothing to stop the elves from getting out on another floor as we had done the first time we'd been using it to escape, but there were only two exits from the mountain currently, and we were going to head toward one of them.

*I'll help seal up the stairs*, Zephyr said as we pulled back into the dimly lit but familiar space. I wasn't going to argue with him, but I didn't hurry away either. Some elves were still hurrying down from above.

"The top way out?" Cherisse asked one of them as an earth elf stepped up to help Zephyr and the elf who had been waiting to open and shut the stairwell as needed.

"Destroyed. They've only got the portal and the main entrance left."

"Good. It won't hold them forever, but hopefully long enough."

I could see Cherisse shaking and a limp in her gait as the stairwell was sealed and we hurried down the steps.

Although I was pretty sure this wasn't going to plan, I was impressed by Cherisse's resolve. She hadn't given up, and she was still encouraging everyone to get where they needed to be.

Zephyr helped me when I stumbled, my body aching and tired. Going through the portal with my mind had taken a fair amount of energy, and I wasn't sure how much more I had. He was less taxed, however, and I was grateful as he used his abilities to get us down the rest of the way.

We came out at a place I recognized, near an old van that had once been used to capture us and bring us to the mountain. We'd exploded the wall at the bottom of the stairwell out and into it. Someone had begun repairing it since then, but it still showed some signs of damage.

I was going past it and waiting for the others to get out of the way before I thought about what I was doing. As soon as Zephyr and the other two earth elves had the stairwell closed up, I moved the van with the air and plonked it down right over the exit.

A wry grin crossed Zephyr's face, then we looked around the room. Every elf who lived in the mountain, along with every gnome, dwarf, and mythical, was standing in the large area. Most of them clutched belongings, and I realized my away bag was still in the mountain and I hadn't been given a chance to go get it.

Although the most valuable items I had were safe at the warehouse, some of the items in it were important to me. First was the communication stone to Ronan and everything I'd been given at the Sanctuary the last time I was there, including one of the boxes Laeroth had made.

I was wondering if there was any way I could sneak up to it when the elf who'd brought me breakfast each day pushed through the crowd. He had the familiar-looking bag slung over his shoulder.

"I knew you wouldn't want to leave this behind when it was all you'd come with," he said.

I blinked before nodding, a lump of gratitude in my throat.

"I can call for backup with what's in here," I said.

"Then do so. We're going to need it," he replied, barely above a whisper.

## CHAPTER FIFTEEN

While Cherisse and Simon took a roll call and checked they had everyone, I gave Zephyr a pointed look and found a space to sit on the floor away from prying eyes. I then pulled out the communication stone to Ronan and activated it.

At first, nothing happened, but the stone grew warmer, and I feared that Ronan wouldn't have picked up on my request to commune with him across the distances or that it had somehow broken or been blocked.

Finally, my mind left my body and entered the space Ronan's mind was in.

"You look troubled, Henera," Ronan said as soon as we'd bowed to each other.

I nodded and quickly told him of what had happened and my fears for the mountain. It needed to be held and the dark elves pushed back, but right now, there were a lot of wounded and tired cult elves trying to defend against them alone.

"I will inform Minsheng immediately and go to the council as well. I'm sure we can send aid. The organization and soldiers of this country are also likely to have useful resources."

Ronan's take-charge attitude and calm response helped me feel better as well and surer I could get through this. Whatever was coming or had come through the portal, we needed to hold them back until the cavalry arrived.

I answered his questions on military-style matters. Numbers, what the elves were capable of, and what we had to work with here. Sadly I had no good answers to some of his questions, but I did my best and tried not to worry about the rest.

I was back in the large cavern, and I could hear Cherisse giving orders again. The dark elves had begun to work out where we were and that we blocked their way. While we could hold them here for a while, I was pretty sure that we couldn't hold it forever.

I was getting to my feet and tucking the communication stone away when Cherisse stormed around Roth, his body having been shielding me from sight. Her eyes went straight to the stone.

"Have you been spying on us?" she demanded.

"No. I have been asking for backup. Elves from my teams and the Sanctuary. Probably soldiers who are used to fighting elves as well." I held her gaze, trying to keep calm despite the glare on her face. It wasn't going to help if I also got angry and lashed out.

"We don't need backup. We can defend this mountain and push them back."

"Maybe, but maybe not, and we can't afford to be wrong."

She growled, but she didn't argue further.

Before I could suggest we do anything else, there was a yell from the elevator shaft, and I got the feeling the first of the air elves was on their way. I reached into my pack for the spare snacks I always had stashed in it and tore into the first candy bar I found. I had a feeling I was going to need plenty more energy before this day was over.

Thankfully, I wasn't the only one who had thought of this, and food was being handed out in multiple other ways, the vehicles yanked open and revealing stashes of provisions. More were in crates near the entrance, and I noticed a lot on trolleys and carts. It was clear that they'd prepared for this as well.

While I wasn't happy that we'd lost control of part of the mountain, I was grateful that had been thought of. Leaving Zephyr, Roth, and Sen to watch the stairwell but taking Nuri with me, I made my way through the crowds to join the other elves at the elevator shaft.

I could feel the presence of the dark elves in the shaft as I got closer, their minds feeling outward and over the room. I wasn't sure anyone else could feel their creeping minds, several of them doing what I had essentially been doing on their side of the portal and trying to work out numbers and where we were.

I took control of the air in a blanket over the crowds and pushed their minds back until I had the upper hand and they couldn't tell where we were or how many there were. It wasn't going to delay them much, but it was a small way I could rebel against what they were doing, and it had the potential to save lives.

Although I didn't want to kill anyone, Cherisse and several other elves didn't agree with this strategy. They were soon blasting these elves around and stealing the air holding them up.

Briefly reaching into the bottom of the elevator shaft, I felt the broken and twisted metal box at the bottom, barely recognizable and a health hazard. There was a good chance that any elf who fell on top of that was not going to live for very long afterward. If they survived the fall.

It wasn't easy to slow a descent with air, and I'd had some rough landings of my own, but in a small shaft, it would be even worse. It was going to be almost certain death. Yet the elves in the elevator shaft fought on, and more of them appeared. They were trying to reach out and find out what they faced, but I kept blocking them at every turn, not wanting to do anything aggressive and have their deaths on my hands, despite being aware that they wouldn't be likely to afford me the same courtesy.

Within minutes they realized they were in trouble, however, and soon one of them crashed downwards, the air stolen from them. The other dark elves helped, and I didn't block them this time or get in the way.

Once more, however, I didn't need to. The elves around me blocked the air in the shaft and stopped the other air elves from being able to do anything. It was brutal, and I winced as several of them died.

The skirmish in the elevator shaft didn't last much longer before the dark elves either gave up or decided they'd gotten what they came for and made their way back to the top of the mountain. I was relieved and sat back, leaning against another crate of food while Simon came over to me.

"I hear from Cherisse that you've called in some back-up," he said, no other words of introduction.

With a nod, I explained who I thought would come to our rescue and why. I also made it clear that they'd want to push back into the mountain and probably close the portal if they could.

"Cherisse won't like that. And besides, making new pillars isn't easy. There aren't many who know how, let alone have the skill."

Frowning, I didn't reply. I hadn't thought about that part of it. I didn't know how to make a pillar. All I knew was that they had a crystal in them and runes carved over the outside. I also knew that some magic had been used from the four items and great relics I wore. I didn't know if the minor relic I had recently been given might be usable instead of using the great artifacts from my powerful ancestors, but I didn't want to pin my hopes on that chance.

Something needed to change to ensure this portal was protected, but I had no idea what that could be yet. I could feel the tension in the room as Simon talked about closing the portal. It was clear that a lot of the elves around me wanted it open. Cherisse might have some crazy ideas and hopes, but she wasn't alone in holding them.

I backed up from everyone, grateful when Simon dropped the conversation and organized the air elves into a schedule to keep an eye on the elevator shaft so that as many elves as possible could rest. Feeling the familiar tug in my stomach that meant Zephyr was too far away from me, made worse by Sen and Roth being with him, I returned to his side.

The stairwell was silent. Cherisse had organized a team of earth elves similarly to Simon. They were taking shifts, and many were resting.

There was no part of me that could relax, however. I wanted to be sure that the elves weren't getting out, and there was still another exit that had only been blocked. There was also the tunnel to the sea. Nothing was stopping the dark elves from getting out through those routes right now.

"We need to set up some scouts to make sure they stay in the mountain," I said a moment later.

"I have far more interest in retaking the mountain than ensuring none get out. If they want to spread themselves thin to find a way out, then let them. I'm going to focus on getting that portal back. Of course, as always, feel free to do as you please. You seem to anyway."

The anger in Cherisse's voice made me want to thump her. I hadn't brought this attack on us, and other portals needed protecting as well. If the elves got out, there was a chance they'd find some of the others. Or hurt humans and divide the world again, or any number of other scenarios that could ruin us.

I didn't have much to work with, however. I and my four mythicals couldn't monitor both exits. As Cherisse stormed off to give more orders, however, a couple of earth elves came up to me.

"We've not been instructed to help with anything. We could help you," the guy said, his eyes alight.

"Won't that get you into hot water?" I asked, although I had no desire to put them off.

"Maybe, but you're right. We can't let them get out of this mountain, and if we can take out more of them while they think we're focused elsewhere, so be it. We'll need some air elves to make sure they don't get out the top of the mountain ideally, but there is a trail up there."

"I'll help," Simon said, his voice coming from over my shoulder.

I jumped as I turned, not having noticed him approaching.

There was a huge part of me that wanted to say no simply because of who he was, but we needed the help. He was also one of the few I was sure could help me without incurring too much wrath from Cherisse.

*And you technically have permission from her to do this*, Zephyr pointed out.

I fought back a chuckle and nodded. Help was needed too much for me to turn Simon down. We needed to turn this situation around, and I was grateful we had allies until the cavalry arrived.

As soon as I gave Simon the go-ahead, he called another couple of elves closer, both of them air elves by the pattern on the robes they wore. I was worried that air and earth elves alone weren't going to be enough, but we needed these two elements for monitoring the two escape routes, if nothing else.

We spent the next half-hour sitting in a corner, going over what Simon and the others knew of the layout of the whole mountain inside and out and how best we could defend it from anyone who might get out of the mountain.

I looked over the scrawled drawings and notes and knew this wasn't going to be easy to defend with how few we had. I had to hope that we could survive until more help arrived. Or that Cherisse could push back enough to retake the portal.

With a plan, I opted to take the first watch in the air with Zephyr, knowing that we could fly and keep an eye on the outside of the mountain more easily. While everyone else was drained and Zephyr could keep us in the air, it was the best use of our abilities. It would also incur the least wrath from Cherisse for now. And that was worth having.

We left Roth, Sen, and Nuri to rest as well and took to the skies. Although I didn't like being far from my mythicals, someone had to stay in the mountain so we could let Simon know if there was a problem, and it ought to be a mythical I could trust.

Of course, there was a chance that Simon wouldn't be able to get help to me in time, but it concerned me less than the other possible outcomes.

Morphing into dragon form, Zephyr stretched out. It was an impressive feat to witness, and it made me marvel at the strength in him. I had been truly blessed the day Zephyr had bonded with me and become my dragon.

Once I was in the air, I felt better. The outside of the mountain was lit up by the evening sun. So much of the day had disappeared in a haze of fighting and trying to survive. It also took a lot longer to go through the portal and back than I anticipated. But I had to make sure I fought back against the dark elf and learned what I could.

As we climbed in the air, Zephyr's powerful wings taking us higher, my calmness returned. The familiar tug in my stomach of my mythicals being somewhere else was disconcerting, but I was leaving them somewhere safer for now. And it was never quite as bad as being away from Zephyr felt.

Having entered the mountain from the outside up here on a previous occasion, Zephyr knew where he was heading, and we touched down on the side of the mountain not far from it. I could see the path he'd followed the first time we'd been on the mountain. I'd been inside and trapped, and he had spent several days on the outside.

I had watched through his eyes as he'd snuck inside the building and taken out an elf controlling the door. There was no door to the outside now, just a pile of rubble. It blocked the route and wouldn't be easy to move, even for an earth elf. But it wasn't impossible to move either.

As soon as we were there on the side of the mountain, we found somewhere out of the way to hide. I reached through the rubble with my mind, finding air spaces and creeping my mind deeper though I could have connected to the rock as well. It was a fun challenge, and it would drain me less to only be connected to one element for a while.

With Zephyr's warm body pressed against my side in his dragon form, keeping the wind off, I wasn't that cold. Night up here would be unpleasant, and I made a mental note to bring supplies up if we thought this was going to last more than one day.

*We can always set a fire going somewhere they are unlikely to notice,* Zephyr said. *Or get Nuri to join us.*

I considered the possibilities but opted to do nothing. A part of me hoped that Minsheng would arrive with extra support soon. It would give me more to work with and make it easier to push the dark elves back if Cherisse hadn't managed to already.

# CHAPTER SIXTEEN

Several hours later I stomped my cold, numb feet to get some feeling into them. The day had given way to night, and the air around us had grown cooler until I was sure I would freeze if I didn't decide to do something.

*Stay here and keep watch*, Zephyr said before leaping into the air and flying off again. I was blasted by cold air and wind, his body no longer shielding me from the weather.

I hastily threw up an air barrier and heated it by combining it with my fire elemental powers. It worked, but I wasn't as practiced using fire, and it was going to drain me if I kept it up all night, especially as I was the only one monitoring the inside of the mountain so far.

Now and then, we'd felt the presence of another elf or two in the background as if they were scouting the insides of the place and getting to know where everything was. They'd done this more than once, but that had been nearer the beginning of our watch, and since then, we'd felt nothing. That wouldn't last.

The tunnel on the inside naturally led to a pile of rubble

and had been blocked. The elves had examined the inside of the blockage a couple of times. I'd pulled back as they'd approached each time, but I'd made sure I could detect them and their wandering minds until the threat had gone away.

Zephyr returned before too long, a broken tree trunk in his hands.

*I think it's been dead long enough that it should burn, but it might need encouragement*, he said as he landed. He used his claws to break it up into more manageable chunks. I floated some into a pile while using my hands to position them into a good shape for a fire. It was far too much wood to burn at once, but the others would appreciate it if we were up here for a long time.

I shifted the rock to make a three-sided enclosure and then moved the spare wood into it, setting it back so it would be mostly out of the rain and wind. Finally, I finished the fire and used my abilities to heat some smaller branches and twigs so much they caught alight.

I marveled at what I'd achieved and created, but I also appreciated the warmth and checked that it couldn't easily be detected from inside the mountain. Just in case, Zephyr moved between it and the tunnel so his large form blocked the light.

Feeling warmer in no time, I sighed and reached into my pack to snack some more. I was grateful we'd brought up some food with us but it wasn't enough to feed Zephyr by a long way.

*It's okay. I ate another mountain goat while I was looking for a dead tree*, he said.

My eyes met his as I worked out if he was serious or

not. I couldn't be sure, but I also didn't know if I wanted to be sure one way or another. Although I wanted him to eat, I worried that it wasn't the most conventional way to get sustenance.

*They were wild,* he added. *Don't worry. We don't owe some farmer any money or anything.*

I grinned as Zephyr brought his head nearer the fire and me. Leaning into him I continued to snack and monitor the inside of the building. I was still chewing on the last mouthful when I thought I felt movement.

Concentrating, feeling out farther toward it, I slowly got to my feet. Zephyr sensed the change and also got to his feet, his gaze going to the tunnel. In dragon form, he couldn't use my abilities, but he waited patiently for me to walk closer and focus.

I could feel the air moving at the very edge of my reach, deep in the mountain, but I couldn't make out the shapes as easily from where I was. Although I made the movements out and what was going where I didn't have to concentrate for much longer before the form of several dark elves came closer.

There was a group of ten of them, in double file, coming down the corridor like a marching army. I quickly told Zephyr what I saw, but I stopped him from taking human form.

*We might need to fly from them, and I think it's better to have your gas.*

*I'm more rested than you.*

*I know, but there's only ten of them, and they've got to get out to us first.*

He sighed but nodded. It was the best course of action,

even if it wasn't what he wanted to do. I appreciated his concern and desire to fight alongside me, but for now, we needed to hold his abilities in reserve.

At first, the ten elves reached the dead-end and stopped to wait, almost as if they expected the rubble to no longer be in their way or didn't know what to do about it. Wondering if I'd missed something, I waited as well, feeling out and around them but not sure what I was supposed to be looking for.

I couldn't detect any other elves, but before long, they stepped forward and took control of the earth and rubble as if they were one person. At the same time, they reached out for each other and linked hands.

It was the strangest use of abilities I'd ever seen. All of them were earth elves, and they were working together to control the same elements. I stood there so stunned by it that I wasn't sure what to do. How was this possible?

*What does it feel like they're doing?* Zephyr asked me. I tried to put it into words, but I had to reach out with my earth ability and see for myself to understand. I could feel the grip of ten elves on the same element. It was strange, as if they'd somehow overlapped their ability with each other and were controlling the element in the same way.

Here on earth, everyone controlled the elements the way their minds were most suited to doing so. And that meant the control conflicted. It happened between me and the other elves in the mountain. The elements were marked, and it was a different way of controlling them, but I still did so my way and not the way another elf did.

As I watched them longer, however, I realized it made sense. If the elves controlled the elements in the same way and learned to do so, then they could effectively adapt to the elements being marked. It meant that Cherisse's worry that the elves on the other side had no way of surviving was entirely unfounded.

I couldn't watch them forever, though. They were pulling apart the rubble, moving it outward, and making the hallway longer. And they were headed right for me.

Taking a deep breath, I took control of the rubble ahead of them where they hadn't reached yet and simply held onto it, wrapping my grip around the elements in a different way to them and making sure the rubble wouldn't budge. At the same time, I packed the rubble in tighter, making it denser and adding to the blockage in front of them.

For a few minutes they continued, oblivious to my control and what was happening before them. Eventually, they reached where I was holding on, however, and it stopped them in their tracks.

I could feel them shuffle awkwardly before they moved and tried again, the ten combined minds pressed against mine. My mind hurt; the barrage was intense and stronger than I'd have hoped to be up against. It wasn't the same as fighting ten elves normally was.

As the pressure increased, I could feel the pain growing, but I continued to hold it against them. I had the impression that if I let go, it would be impossible to stop them from coming forward any farther.

Beside me, Zephyr morphed into human form and then took my hand and reached out with his mind as well.

*Hold on as long as you can. I'm going to help you*, he said.

He explored forward and reached out the way they

were. I wasn't sure it was going to work, but while I gritted my teeth, my whole mind seeming to go numb to everything but the pressure on it and the elements I was locked into holding as tightly as possible, the difficulty eased, and his mind joined me.

It was a strange feeling, and I wasn't sure how it was working exactly, but he slipped into the same pattern as me, and the pressure eased again as he held the rock with me, our power combining as the ten dark elves appeared to be doing.

They suddenly backed off, and I exhaled in relief, my skull pounding. I didn't let go, however, not sure what else was going on, but knowing that I couldn't let them get a chance to take control by losing my focus.

*This feels weird*, Zephyr said when the ten took a step back and waited, still in formation.

We were still combined, and I could feel his mind working with mine, but only in the earth we were holding together. I held the air in the mountain alone, and I could feel him holding more earth around the area I did.

Just as I had been doing before I'd been assaulted by the dark elves, Zephyr was bolstering the defenses further, making the rock denser and closing in more of the gaps. Essentially adding to the workload if the elves were to get out this way.

*Do you think they'll give up?* I asked Zephyr as I ate the last snack bar I had.

*I hope so, but things aren't usually so easy. Normally people underestimate us and we have to stomp on them to get them to understand that no one beats the Henera and her dragon.*

*Good point,* I replied. *You'd think they'd talk to each other and tell each other that it's a waste of time.*

*Or that I'm a cranky dragon and shouldn't be pissed off further.*

*Oh, you're not cranky. Not unless they stop you from getting pizza when you want it.*

*I always want pizza.*

*Who doesn't?*

We chuckled as we waited and watched again. It was weird to be holding back and waiting for someone else to make the next move, but I couldn't waste my energy when we were up against ten dark elves. There was a mountain full of them and a portal that could admit in many more.

If we needed backup, I could swiftly request some since Nuri, Sen, and Roth were near Simon, but ideally, they needed to be resting to take their watch. Although I worried that none of them were going to be able to defend the areas without Zephyr or me to teach them what we'd learned.

I was about to suggest that Zephyr let go and preserve his power when more elves appeared, another group of ten arriving in a similar formation. They divided in two down the middle and came around to flank the elves already there.

While they did, I silently prayed that they would be replacements and not reinforcements, but after the front elf of the new group conversed briefly with the front elf of the old group, they stepped forward again as one unit.

*We might need help,* I said to Zephyr, wanting to get his opinion before I called for the rest of our bonded mythicals to get aid.

*Give it a moment. The first group must be tired. We only need them to begin getting tired again and we'll hold out. And we have no idea if the new ten are as strong.*

I frowned, hoping that Zephyr was right and this was going to be a lot easier than I feared. But the new elves could be stronger. Either way, they began to meld their grip and I knew we were about to find out.

Trying not to worry, I focused on holding my grip in place with Zephyr again. He let go of everything else as the assault began and we were under pressure once more. The pain increased, making it clear this wasn't going to be a pleasant way to hold on for a long time.

Although it hurt, I was sure that it wasn't quite as bad as it had been holding the rocks against the ten elves on my own. Or the pain was something I was getting used to.

I wasn't sure we could keep it up, however, and as the elves dug in deeper and I saw the pain on Zephyr's face as well, I was pretty sure we needed help.

*Help might not come swiftly,* I heard Roth say a moment later, his voice fainter than I'd have liked. *The elves have begun attacking from the elevator shaft and the stairwell. And I believe some have gone down the tunnel to the sea. Several water and earth elves have gone that way to defend the exit, but everyone here is engaged in battle.*

*Do what you can to help, but stay out of serious danger,* I replied, feeling a hint of fear creep into my chest.

It sounded as if there were a lot more dark elves inside the mountain than there had been and more had come through the portal in the time we'd been resting. I hoped there was a finite number of them to come through and we were close to that limit because I only had so many people coming to back us up in battle.

I gritted my teeth as the twenty dark elves pushed harder and made the pain grow further.

*Slip back*, Zephyr suggested. *See if we can make them fight hard and drain them and then put it back when they're done and have to give up.*

No part of me liked the idea, but we couldn't stand up against the pain much longer and he was right that having a strategy was important.

I agreed and we retreated, giving the elves something to work with. They pulled the rock and earth we'd been holding there out of the way, and I sighed. It was so quickly moved clear that it only bought us a minute or so before we were locked in a battle over the next section.

The respite had allowed the pain to fade, however, and it had drained the elves in front of us of some of their power. At least I hoped it had.

We continued to hold on again for several more minutes before we agreed to make another strategic retreat mentally and then waited as they used their abilities to move more rock and drained themselves further.

I had no idea for sure how these elves recharged their abilities, but given they slept the same way elves here did, I was pretty sure they also ate and would need to spend some time recuperating as anyone else would have to.

Either way, if this continued, it was going to be a long night. We couldn't give in, and they didn't appear to be tiring or slowing down.

# CHAPTER SEVENTEEN

As time wore on in this dangerous game of attempting to wear each other down, I almost gave up several times. Sen, Roth, and Nuri were keeping us updated with what was happening elsewhere, and I was slowly giving more ground on top of the mountain with Zephyr.

My mind was beginning to grow weaker, the pressure mounting to an almost insane level. We'd given back over half of the remaining rubble in the way as well and what was left was less compact and would be easier for them to break through. On top of that, the elves didn't seem to be running out of power. All twenty were still driving forward.

*We need a new plan,* I said to Zephyr as we gave another section and the pain lessened. It wasn't ideal to be trying anything without backup, but Nuri and Roth had assured me that none could come right now.

*Can you make a wall behind them quickly? Doesn't have to be big, just behind them and not let any air out.*

A grin spread across my face at the idea and I quickly

got to work, not sure why Zephyr wanted it but feeling his mind move and then grab control of more earth as well.

While we weren't being challenged for control of the next section we quickly got to work, and then Zephyr's control slipped away from being combined with mine, leaving me holding the path alone.

*You won't have to hold it long,* Zephyr said as he morphed into a dragon beside me.

It took a while, his mind tired from everything else and no doubt feeling the pain I did as well, but the twenty elves were beginning to pressure me when Zephyr stepped forward, put his dragon mouth against a small hole he had made, and exhaled into the small room the earth elves were trapped in.

The effect was almost instant as they were enveloped in a thick cloud of Zephyr's paralyzing gas weapon. I almost laughed aloud as they fell over like dominoes. The few at the back tried to retreat, only to discover that there was a wall blocking them into the space, and there was nowhere to go and no way to get away from the gas.

A couple of them tried to attack the wall I'd made on the other side, but I switched my focus to holding onto it, and within seconds, the elves were out cold.

*Make the wall thicker and close this gap on this side for now,* Zephyr said.

*Okay. Stay in dragon form and save your power. It feels like they need us back at the bottom of the mountain.*

*Maybe,* Zephyr replied, but I could feel his reluctance to hold back and stay in dragon form.

I could understand it as well. I wouldn't want to do

nothing, especially when he was far better with earth than I was and it was earth work.

Despite that, I did my best and soon had the holes filled in and the twenty elves locked in with Zephyr's gas and the thickest walls I could manage around them. I stopped when I wobbled, light-headed, and feeling the bonds with my mythicals take a hit. I couldn't keep on any longer or I ran the risk of not being able to feel Sen, Roth, and Nuri.

Trying not to panic about the idea of rushing into another battle on so little energy, I climbed up onto Zephyr's back and let him fly me down the mountain. It would leave the top route unguarded for a while, but I was pretty sure any elves that tried to rescue the trapped twenty would just knock themselves out for a while, and the ones in there were going to be out cold for the better part of half a day even with the swifter elf metabolism.

In short, we were fine for now.

I could feel Sen, Roth, and Nuri as we flew down the mountain and toward the main entrance. Roth had moved to the tunnel toward the sea. I could feel him channeling water and generally kicking ass. Nuri and Sen were still inside the mountain, and I briefly let myself see what Sen could, the small myconid's view the one I found easiest to connect with and process.

She was standing on Simon's shoulder blasting ice darts at a dark elf to keep it from doing anything while Simon pinned another two down with air blasts. They were standing near the stairwell and I could make out the movement of other elves there trying to stem what appeared to be a flood of attackers.

I got Zephyr to take us as close as possible to that

section of the entrance and slid off his back as soon as he was close to the ground. I ran for the nearest crate of food and an elf near it anticipated my desire, grabbing a candy bar from it and tearing it open.

As soon as I was close enough, they handed it to me and grabbed another to rip the top.

I grinned as I munched, and the elf explained what had been happening as if I was expected and this was normal.

"We've gotten the elevator mostly sorted still. Eight of our best elves knocking the air out from under any that come too close. Made them wary of sending many elves that way. They work as a team in a strange way and often kicking the control of one or making one come crashing down collapses the entire group of dark elves."

"Yeah, I think I know why but I'll explain that later," I replied in between bites of food.

"There's some commotion down at the sea tunnel. They've broken out of the side of that and come around to attack us from behind. Cherisse led a charge that way with some more water and earth elves, plus that horse of yours."

"Pegasus," Zephyr said, his deep rumble echoing around the small area we were in.

I could see the shock on the young elf's face as he corrected himself. I grinned and started on the second bar of chocolate. It wasn't that big a deal, but I was glad that my mythicals were standing up for themselves without me needing to.

"And the stairs?" Zephyr asked a moment later, his voice quieter and gentler again.

"That's where the main fight is. They've gotten a lot of

elves, and they're doing things with magic we've never seen before."

"A new enemy always does," I replied as I shoved another chunk of chocolate into my mouth.

I held out my hand to take another set of candy bars before striding toward the sounds of fighting and the feel of Sen and Nuri. I wasn't sure I wanted to eat any more chocolate, already feeling sick, but I wasn't going to deny my body some quick energy and food when there was a battle to fight.

Thankfully a woman ran up with a bottle of water, unscrewing the cap and then giving it to me as I strode closer. Zephyr lingered behind before he took human form once more and also grabbed a candy bar.

I noticed the looks on the faces around us, many not used to seeing something like that. We made our way through the vehicles, injured elves and everyone else running back and forth as Simon issued commands.

It was clear the dark elves were pushing hard, but I quickly flew up and counted them. There were fewer of them than us, but they were fighting in units of like-minded elementals, and that was incredibly contradictory to the cult's tactics. Cherisse had her elves teaming up in sets of four different elements so she had fighting groups who could collectively do anything.

This wasn't going to work as effectively against a set of dark elves who were operating as single units of people.

I blasted a couple of unsuspecting elves off their feet, however, and felt them give way, whatever they were doing halted as I continued to pin them down with air like Simon was doing with others.

Although I wasn't sure what to do next, I moved closer to Simon, forming a protective arc around a group of cult elves who had fought so hard they were out of magic despite the food.

Knowing how easy it was to run out of energy, I hesitated near them to get a read on the situation. I'd assumed this was going to be a fairly easy fight, but there were a lot of cult elves beginning to tire. I wasn't in great shape either.

*We can only do our best*, Zephyr pointed out.

*True, but we need to push these elves back before it's too late. And we're running out of options.*

*I'm pretty sure I can't gas these ones too.*

*Nope, not without you switching back yet again and this whole room going with them.*

I frowned, but I didn't stop trying to push the elves back. The dark elves were doing as feared and teaming up in small units to control the elements. I snatched control of air, fire, water, or earth as I came across anything aggressive, but it wasn't easy, and I was soon tired again.

Zephyr backed me up, doing the same, and slowly we helped the elves around us get back on their feet and into a line of defense. It wasn't a perfect plan, but it was taking energy from the dark elves and giving the elves on my side some support.

I could see their gratitude as I helped one older woman back to her feet and blocked a blast of air meant for a guy defending three other elves. Zephyr moved with me, doing similar, targeting specific areas and fights where our presence and skill could quickly turn a smaller fight back in a different direction.

Within minutes it was turning the tide overall, and the elves were regrouping around Simon to drive the dark elves back. Around me were several dead dark elves, some of them burned and others lying at strange angles near rocks or vehicles, their bodies broken. It made me sick, but it had become a kill or be killed fight.

I wanted to make it stop, my head beginning to feel fuzzy again, but I couldn't give up and I couldn't let it get to me. Not this time.

*We'll be okay, Aella. Just keep focusing on pushing them back. Help will be here soon, and we'll keep everyone safe.* Zephyr's words rumbled, calming me once more.

I didn't know how he could keep so calm in battles, but I was grateful that he could. As the earth under my feet reached up to lock on, I reminded myself to focus and snatched control away. A group of four earth-based dark elves reeled backward as my mind slammed into theirs.

Simon and a couple of air elves with him seized the opportunity and blasted the organized group backward into the wall. There was a sickening crunch and the two at the back went limp. The front two were more cushioned, but they still didn't move, dazed, pained expressions on their faces.

More dark elves came out of the stairwell, however, forming a defensive perimeter into the room that I had no idea how to breach. I made my way to Simon's side, working into his group and helping to push the dark elves back.

"We're running out of oomph," he said quietly to me as we were pushed back again.

I frowned as I bumped into another of the vehicles in

the room. Most of them had moved and the food crates over here were mostly empty except for wrappers and drained bottles. Taking a massive swig of water, I tried to think of something we could do, but the elves around the base of the stairwell were relentless.

It was as if they cared nothing for their lives. Where I had thought the cult was well trained, these units of like-minded elves were so much more powerful and coordinated. We might have been defending our home, but they had prepared to take it from us.

Despair filled me, but I blasted them back with as much air as I could, holding the line and trying to work out how to push them back farther. They resisted me and challenged my control of the air as I cycled it, pushing down and back.

Zephyr grabbed control of the earth and began raising a new barrier, penning them in. I could see the strain on his face as more of the dark elves challenged him as well, but neither of us stopped or gave up.

The pain grew as Zephyr took my hand, the barrier he'd created a significant hurdle. I was feeling my mind start to fuzz and knew that I was beginning to lose momentum when I heard the roar of engines and the whine of a large helicopter above the din. There was cheering and yelling coming from the main entrance.

"Hold on a little longer," Simon yelled beside me before pushing through the crowd.

Someone else shoved another unwrapped candy bar in my hand and more elves joined me, hurling as much air as they could. At the same time, the barrier Zephyr was creating grew and became thicker.

Before I could work out what was happening outside for sure, but my heart hopeful that it was Minsheng or some soldiers, or any ally, my powers gave out, Zephyr and I unable to use magic at the same time. My connection to Sen, Roth, and Nuri went with it as I wobbled, light-headed.

Zephyr caught me and hugged me to him as he pulled me back from the fight and behind the large truck near us.

I quickly ate the candy bar, trying to ignore the pain in my head, and leaned into him.

"It's okay," he said as I realized that I was crying. "Help has arrived. Rest here. I'm going to get them in here and get us some guns if nothing else."

I nodded, not wanting him to leave when I couldn't feel our bond but knowing that I didn't have much choice. A gun would mean we could keep fighting.

There was no tug in my stomach as he walked away. The sadness and strangeness I felt not knowing my mythicals were okay. It was a feeling I'd had once before, and I had hated it then.

Simon came back a little later, however, Minsheng and the major with him and Sen on his shoulder. The myconid ran and leaped over to me, narrowly missing being hit by a blast of air.

The cult elves were falling back again as the dark elves tore the barrier down and pushed forward. More soldiers appeared, shooting darts into the crowds of elves with an efficient skill that made me grateful they were allies. The cult elves fell in with the soldiers, protecting them with air barriers and blasting away fire with water.

I sighed with relief as Minsheng pressed a gun into my hands.

"We've got this," he said. "Everyone is here now."

I nodded, noticing a bruise on his arm that hadn't been there before and a cut on the major's face.

"Looks like you've got a story to tell as well," I replied. I took a deep breath and moved to the edge of the vehicle so I could see more of the battle. I climbed up onto the hood and began firing over the heads of the other elves into the crowds.

Although I normally used my abilities to help keep my projectiles on target, I had still practiced plenty without using my power, thanks to Daisy and Ronan. I hit several elves quickly, the dark elves having no idea what was happening.

The unexpected weaponry and the unsure way to defend against it that the dark elves displayed meant that many of the elves near the front were soon out cold and we could start pushing the forces back again.

The familiar tug reappeared in my stomach as Zephyr and I reconnected, and my powers regenerated. Zephyr threw an air barrier up in front of us, his abilities seemingly inexhaustible as long as we were connected.

Although I could feel him, it took a moment longer to feel Sen. She gave my neck a quick snuggle before she sent out more ice darts, hitting some elves that were trying to sneak to one side with them and making them think twice.

Within minutes we'd pushed the elves back, and Roth and Nuri were back in the main cavern, along with Cherisse and the other elves who had been defending the back route out of the stairwell. I raised an eyebrow as I saw the gun in her hands as well and saw her come to my side.

"The soldiers are holding the tunnel," she said, sounding as tired as I felt.

"Let's get this bunch pushed back up then and make them think twice about coming down again," I replied.

She gave me a wry grin, and we turned back to the battle. We fired a few more shots, taking out another elf each, then whoever was in command of the dark elves had them pull back.

The retreat was swifter than any element of the battle had been so far. Elves seemed to melt into the rock and up the stairs. Cherisse and the major were commanding everyone to hold, waiting to see what happened.

Slowly everyone relaxed, some elves sitting down where they stood, everyone weary.

I leaned into Zephyr again, almost dropping the rifle, my hands numb and my body so tired I shook. That had been the worst battle I'd ever been in, and I had a feeling there were more coming.

# CHAPTER EIGHTEEN

After taking painkillers and stuffing my face, I felt normal again. I wasn't the only one walking gingerly around the main cavern. I'd tried to sleep, as many other elves were still doing. When you had an entire mountain's worth of elves with only one large cavern and the tents the soldiers were still setting up outside, it wasn't ideal.

The soldiers and the Sanctuary and warehouse elves were doing everything they could to set up a temporary base outside. I was impressed with how quickly we had something that looked functional, but it was barely enough.

Going outside with the four mythicals at my sides and on my shoulders, I noticed the elves and soldiers giving way to us as if we were royalty. If there had been any animosity between any of them and me before, it was gone now. I'd defended and fought beside everyone here and I'd given everything I had.

There was something about putting your life in danger to defend someone else's life and home that made it easier to get along. Although I noticed there was some tension between the soldiers and Amcika elves, it was less pronounced than I'd feared. As the soldiers shared more provisions and offered beds, blankets, and sleeping space, even Cherisse was showing respect.

I found the cult leader with Simon, Minsheng, the general, the major, Sierrathen, and Ronan in a small tent to one side of the entrance with soldiers, centaurs, and elves guarding it.

Dyneira smiled at me as she pulled back the flap to make it easier for me to go inside with the others. Heads turned to me.

"You look like crap," Daisy said, getting up from a chair near the back where I'd not noticed her.

"A night fighting dark elves will do that," I replied, noticing she also sported a bandage. "You don't look much better. What happened?"

"The dark elf did some more funky stuff at the Texas portal," she explained. "We think we've fixed it for now, though."

I lifted an eyebrow, wondering how they'd managed it.

"Remember that shield device Chris tried to make like the Sanctuary shield?" she asked.

Nodding, I thought back to how they'd tried to get it working the day Amcika had kidnapped me. It had been forgotten about in the aftermath.

"With help from a gnome and dwarf in the Sanctuary who maintain it there, we finally got it working. It's around the Texas portal, both keeping it safe and keeping the dark elf from breaking so much," Daisy grinned as she spoke, and I got the impression that she'd been pretty involved in making it work.

Minsheng coughed and drew my attention to the rest of the group.

"What's the plan?" I asked.

"For now, recover, train, and hold the line," Cherisse replied, although she didn't sound too happy about it.

I'd told them everything I knew of the dark elves before resting, and I was sure that it had been factored into the decision, but I wasn't entirely sure I liked it either. I wanted to get these dark elves out of the mountain and back to the world they had come from.

Holding them inside the mountain was far harder than holding the portal, especially as it meant they could keep bringing fresh elves through the portal. The numbers we had to fight against would grow.

"We need you to show the other elves how to control the exact same element at the same time and how to coordinate what's being done," Minsheng said a moment later.

"I don't know if it's possible for others to do," I replied. "Zephyr and I can talk telepathically. It makes it far easier."

"That just means we have to train harder. If they can do it so can we." Cherisse's mouth set into a thin line.

I studied her face, trying to decide if she was seriously offering me an olive branch and accepting that I was here to help her now. I wasn't sure, but her look never changed, and it was clear she was determined to beat back these elves.

"Okay," I said. "Training it is."

"I'll see what I can do to make the line we're holding more permanent and bolster the defenses," the major said.

"The Sanctuary can aid there," Ronan said with a slight bow. "We have plenty of experience guarding a perimeter, and I believe we have some technology that can warn us when an attack might occur."

"Any help will be gratefully received," Cherisse replied, looking at Ronan and then Sierrathen.

I noticed the Sanctuary council elf hadn't said anything and was standing farther back, but I wasn't going to draw attention to her or put her on the spot. The whole conversation felt awkward and on edge enough as it was.

As the meeting came to a natural end, I left the tent again, feeling Cherisse and Minsheng coming with me and my mythicals. As I stood outside and Cherisse summoned different powerful elementals to us, I realized I'd walked in and been told I needed to train everyone else and then walked out again.

So many thoughts were left bubbling in my head that I didn't feel as if I'd had the chance to say. We were in a precarious position, so much of the mountain exposed and an unknown enemy lingering within. Would they grow? Did we need to attack soon?

I did understand the need to help the elves I called allies attack more effectively, however, and they weren't going to learn unless we showed them how. With that in mind, Zephyr and I spent the next hour showing a small group of elves of each element how we'd combined our control.

It took some of them longer than others, but we moved on as soon as two of each element could understand it and model it for the rest of the group. I appreciated that it was an advanced skill. Any elf who couldn't feel the connection of another elf and reach out to explore that with their mind wouldn't be able to learn this.

Thankfully, after I'd done the four groups, no one asked me to do anything else. I could sit down and watch as the elves worked to teach each other. I hadn't been sitting there long when Minsheng came to my side and sat down as well.

"You're troubled. Tell me what's on your mind, and we'll see what we can do about it," my Shishou said, making me feel better.

I told him of my fears that we were taking too long. That every moment we waited, the elves inside the mountain were getting stronger and might bring reinforcements through from the other side of the portal.

It wasn't ideal not to train either, though. I expressed my frustration that everyone had assumed I would be the one to train those needed. The whole conversation made me sound like a whiny brat, however, and I almost didn't say half of what was on my mind.

"I know I'm this Henera, and I know everyone needs me to step up and help out. To defend this place. But there are times I want to be anything but. I want to run away from the pressure and responsibility. I don't want to see dead elves every time I close my eyes to sleep. And I don't want to lie down each night not sure if I'm going to get to sleep or be woken up to fight again before I'm rested."

"The role you play in this isn't an easy one. And anyone would feel those things at least some of the time. I'd be worried if you didn't," Minsheng said. "People sometimes forget that leaders are as vulnerable and full of doubts and needs as the rest of us. But you're not alone in this. Any time it gets too much, you can say. We'll do what we can to help you just as you help us."

The look in Minsheng's eyes as he spoke made me feel better. His understanding and gentleness made me feel as if the world wasn't so bad after all, but I was still tired. Simon soon came up with several more sets of elves.

"Cherisse said you had something to show us," he said, his eyes studying me and looking between me and Minsheng a couple of times.

I considered asking him to learn from the others, but it would only delay how long it took for the whole of our allies to learn. As much as I wanted to preserve my energy to fight any impending battle, some of my power had to be used to prepare for it as well. On top of that, it was good practice for Zephyr and me.

Zephyr got to his feet and helped me up as well before we merged our control again to show Simon and the air elves with him. It was easier than it had been the last time, and I marveled at how swiftly Zephyr and I could learn something new and put it into practice.

By the time I'd taught the elves Simon had brought to me, the first group had taught another set of elves and were taking a rest. I was considering doing the same when the four elven masters from the sanctuary came walking out from between two tents.

I lifted my eyebrows, certain that I'd never seen the four of them outside of the Sanctuary at once before. Sierrathen, Gwaelon, Erlan, and a couple of other students were with them.

"Would you show us what you've learned as well as the cult elves so we may teach our elves as well?" Sierrathen asked. I saw the hesitation and wariness in her face and look.

"Of course," I replied. "Had I known you were here, I'd have offered sooner. I can think of no better elves than you for me to teach and allow to pass the knowledge on."

This put them at ease and made it clear that although everyone in the camp had fought together in battle and were united, there were still insecurities and questions that if allowed, could divide us. It was going to fall partially on my shoulders to stop that from happening.

*It will fall on our shoulders as well,* Zephyr pointed out. *But it also falls on theirs. Sierrathen did the right thing by coming and asking. She could easily have assumed you didn't wish to teach them and let it fester into resentment.*

*You say that as if you have experience.*

*It wasn't always easy being in a leadership role for the four greats, either. And many leaders who have followed. There's trouble in some form or another for most of them.*

*You're really selling this one today,* I replied, sending a wave of affection with it so Zephyr would know I didn't mind.

*It beats not being bonded and being on the run the whole time, trust me.*

I sent more warmth his way, feeling the tint of sorrow to his words despite his chuckle. None of our lives had been easy, and I was constantly reminded that we were in this together and had a wealth of experience and genetic memories to draw from. We had it easier than our ancestors had.

With this in mind, I threw myself into training the masters as they had frequently done for me. I wanted them to have the knowledge I possessed and I wanted us to be able to drive back these dark elves. That meant training.

As soon as they picked it up, I moved on, however. My head hurt, reminding me that I had pushed myself hard the previous day. If the elves attacked, I wouldn't have much to defend the others with.

That didn't mean I had to rest as such, however. Physically, I still had plenty of energy, and my mythicals had done a lot of standing around.

Taking a moment to let Minsheng know where we'd be, I encouraged my mythicals into the air and scooped up Sen. I then led them to the outside of the mountain to a section where we could test our abilities and work together on attacks and defenses. Now more than ever, the five of us needed to be a team. There were plenty of ways we could train that didn't deplete my power in the same way.

Time slipped by as we worked together, my mythicals stronger now that they had more elements open to them. I'd noticed Sen had gained abilities as I'd gained elements, and it was clear from the steam Roth could create that our unique bonded situation changed what they were capable of, but Zephyr in dragon form was still bound only to use his gas weapon as far as we were aware.

Although he had the small dagger attached to one of his horns and it allowed him some basic vine control, it wasn't the full use of the earth element.

It made me think as Nuri blasted past us on fire and catching the ice darts Sen was chucking.

*Do you think you could use other elements in dragon form?* I asked Zephyr as I thought back through our battles. His gas weapon had been set on fire more than once and it would be useful if he could breathe fire, but I also wondered what it would be like if he could incorporate earth or water into his attacks or defense somehow.

*I think I can use water and earth better in dragon form,* he said a moment later. *I've noticed that I don't need to drink in dragon form anymore. It's as if I am absorbing it from the world around me. I've also noticed that sometimes my body seems at one with the earth, and it's easier to move across the ground.*

As Zephyr spoke, I realized it made sense. I had been thinking about purely fight-based advantages, but he was right in that some of the ways our powers could be used was to make our lives better in other aspects. He was more resilient and tired less easily than before. That was useful in everyday life.

*It's understandable you'd focus on abilities that might aid us in battle. We're almost always in battle in one way or another,* Zephyr added.

I couldn't argue with him, but it was a sad reflection of what our life was like that we thought about fighting and if what we were learning could be used in a battle before anything else.

Peace eluded us no matter how much we sought it. It was a sad truth that was beginning to haunt me. When would we finally be done with war?

CHAPTER NINETEEN

When another day dawned, I finally felt more like my usual self. The dark elves had left us alone for an entire day in terms of major attacks. They'd needed to be held back from tunneling out of the top of the mountain again, but a quick trip up there, with some backup from another couple of earth elves, had soon stopped them again.

We'd also made it harder for them to get out that way and soldiers and elves were monitoring the area around the clock.

Grateful for our allies and the break they could get us, I made my way to the massive tent being used as a canteen. Daisy was sitting with Ronan and discussing something.

Before them were drawings and schematics of techno-logical devices I had no clue about. Minsheng joined us, and I listened as the three of them discussed whether something would work to act as a shield or if it would need too big a power supply.

I had no idea what they were talking about, nor what was so interesting about it, beyond the usefulness in battle.

Before I could begin to wrap my head around it, a familiar voice spoke behind me.

"I might be able to help," Chris said. I whirled to face him as Daisy did the same.

I didn't know what to say or do. Although he had been living in the mountain and I'd known he was there, I'd not wanted to seek him out, and I'd known that he wasn't a major part of the operation being run. But that didn't mean the others felt the same.

"As long as that's all you intend to do," Minsheng replied.

Chris held his hands up.

"I know you feel betrayed by me, and we aren't going to agree on what I did. For the most part, I still feel as if I did the right thing. Aella is the Henera, but I do still care enough about this world and the people in it to want to help where I can."

"Then help and save some of them," Daisy replied and shifted over.

I shuffled to the side as well and let him sit between us, my emotions all over the place enough for me to know it wasn't wise of me to say anything. This couldn't be easy on Minsheng either, but if he was willing to curb his feelings and tolerate Chris being here for the sake of others, I could do no different.

By the time my mythicals and I had finished eating, it was clear that the device they were working on was far too complicated for me to understand, but if they got it working, it would make it easier to defend the mountain.

Leaving them to their task and deciding to put myself to better use elsewhere instead of asking for an explanation for something I might never comprehend, I went to find the elven masters to train with or to see how the others were progressing with learning to cooperate like the dark elves were.

On the way, I found Cherisse, Simon, Sierrathen, Ronan, and Gwaelon sitting under a large tree with several books in front of them. As soon as Ronan spotted me, he inclined his head and drew the attention of the rest of the group.

Gwaelon held out an arm and gestured for me to join them. Wondering what they could need from me and what they were discussing but grateful that the two groups were trying to get along, I hurried in their direction.

Roth, Nuri, and Sen happily flopped down in the shade near Ronan, the pegasus matching the half-sitting and half-lying posture Ronan often adopted at meetings. Zephyr was in human form, and he sat down beside me.

"Sierrathen and Gwaelon have kindly brought some books with them that talk of the dark elf and what he is capable of," Simon explained.

While I noticed he seemed genuinely pleased about this, Cherisse smiled politely, the expression never reaching her eyes or making her look anything more than irritated at needing it.

"What do I need to know that I don't?" I asked, wanting to get this meeting over and done with but keep it focused on our common enemy at the same time.

"I've mentioned that he forces his control of the elements unnaturally, haven't I?" Simon replied.

"Yes, although that in itself seems strange. But it would explain why all the elements around him feel similar."

"It appears as if he has forced them to keep his body going. He has lived so long because he can harness all the elements and essentially...repair himself." Sierrathen swallowed as she finished speaking, and I could see the fear this made her feel.

I didn't know what to say. I'd never seen Sierrathen look afraid before. But it was also one of the times I'd seen her away from the Sanctuary, and she wasn't likely to be as relaxed away from the haven.

*You know, if he can do that, we might be able to as well,* Zephyr pointed out while Simon was picking up a book and showing me some of the handwriting inside.

I couldn't read the elvish script very well and my elvish still left a lot to be desired, but I got the gist of it and focused on translating it in my mind while I processed what Zephyr had said to me. Did having access to all the elements make it so we could live forever?

"If you think about it, it actually makes some sense," Simon continued, although I noticed Cherisse shot him a brief glare. "The initial great elementals couldn't kill him. They tried, and collectively they should have been far more powerful than one elf. But they couldn't heal themselves the way he could."

"As long as he had power left, he could heal himself as fast as they could hurt him," I said, starting to understand. "So they put him in a box they thought he couldn't get out of essentially to go crazy or give up and kill himself, maybe even let himself die."

"That seems to be what happened." Gwaelon frowned as he spoke, but the atmosphere changed as I had mentioned what no one else had dared and he was the only one who had been willing to talk afterward.

While this was news that had some bearing on how I might fight this dark elf, what it told me so much more was how screwed up this whole process had been in the first place.

"Why wasn't this common knowledge?" I asked, feeling anger rising inside me. "Why didn't Amcika know that he was capable of this?"

"None of us knew he was capable of this," Gwaelon said, his voice gentle as he reached for my hand.

I wanted to pull back and lash out at someone. It made no sense that no one knew of this. It was one of the most important things to know about the dark elf. He could heal himself. Regenerate and essentially live forever.

Not only did it make what Amcika had done opening the portal obviously foolish, but it meant that if anyone was going to stop the dark elf, they had to fight him down to no power left and then kill him. Or somehow kill him in one hit. Something impossible when he could control the elements well enough that I didn't think I could defeat him, and I was more powerful than any elf who had ever lived otherwise.

It was insane. United, we could not defeat the dark elf. That was without allowing for the army of elves that served him.

Feeling scared, I sat back to think about what to do with the information.

*We should do what we've always done,* Zephyr said. *Learn from it. It will also make us harder to kill.*

*As long as we have the power for it.* I shuddered as I

thought about running out two days earlier. I hadn't been pushed that hard in a long time and it had felt awful.

"Thank you for letting me know this," I said when I realized everyone else was still staring at me. They relaxed, but Sierrathen reached for the book again and flicked to another page.

"There's more in here about the box prison he was put into and how it works. I've had a copy made and left in the Sanctuary. We're trying to reconstruct it and see if we can buy ourselves more time again."

I listened as Simon took an interest and they talked about ancient ways of elven construction. It was clear that some details were missing and the book alluded to knowledge the dwarves had.

I was frustrated. I did not think it wise to put the dark elf back into a box again and leave him there, and I was pretty sure that we didn't have the information to do so easily. It was as if whoever trapped him the first time didn't think it would be so many thousands of years before the Henera came along.

Or that they thought the dark elf would kill himself and save everyone the trouble.

The more I thought about it, the more I pitied him. He had no respect for life and others, but putting him in a box for millennia by himself was a whole new level of low. It made me hurt for him. Did anyone deserve that kind of punishment?

*It was their only option.* There was a sadness in Zephyr's voice.

*Truly?*

*The only one they could think of. They tried everything and almost died so many times.*

*I don't want it to be our only option. We are going to stop this dark elf.*

*Yes, because you're Henera, and you have the same abilities he does. You have something else on top of those that he never will.*

*What's that?* I asked, leaning into Zephyr and looking up at him.

*Love.*

I blinked, feeling the warmth my mythicals radiated toward me, and was unable to speak. They loved me, and I loved them.

But was love going to make the difference? I had to hope it would. Or give up now.

*Love, hope, and faith,* Nuri added. *We have all three. We will defeat him this time.*

I exhaled and nodded. Yes, we would.

"Don't worry about the prison," I said out loud a moment later. Every head turned to stare at me. "We're not going to need it, and it clearly didn't work well enough."

Simon's mouth fell open, but Ronan and Gwaelon grinned and gave the book no more of their attention.

After a moment, Sierrathen nodded but Cherisse shook her head.

"We'll explore every avenue open to us. I want to get my mountain back, and if that means I have to lure him into a prison again and shove him back through the portal myself, I intend to."

"So be it. But know that I intend to finish this once and for all. I will save as many lives as I can and I'll work with you to do so, but this ends. No more stopgaps, no more fighting between us. We're going to defeat the dark elf, and we're going to free everyone who needs freeing."

I didn't give any of them a chance to say anything in response but got up. As I did I noticed that a large black vehicle had pulled up, coming up the road from the perimeter the Mexican soldiers had made around us. None of them had been willing to aid us in the fight, and the US government hadn't tried very hard to persuade them, instead sending in their soldiers.

A small part of me had wondered how the US government had wrangled that one politically, but the general had said something about it being in the best interests of both countries, given there was another portal in Texas and the fight was currently in Mexico.

I wasn't going to argue with where our support came from as long as we had it. In that frame of mind, I wandered toward the newcomers, hoping to greet them and find out what they wanted.

Several men and women got out, primly dressed in suits and one of them carrying a very large, black briefcase. As Iris stepped out I realized it must be people from the organization.

Nuri flew off my shoulder to get Minsheng as I walked closer and smiled purposefully at Iris. The first time we'd met, she'd appeared angry and irritated, but she beamed now.

"Aella-Faye, the Mexican sun suits you, as do the mythicals. Let me introduce you to these members of the organization. We've come here to see who we can help since it's clear the purpose of our organization is finally coming to fruition."

I lifted an eyebrow at how excited she was, but I let myself be steered and guided toward the other three. I took their names in and noticed the briefcase was attached to one of them by handcuffs.

"It looks as if you have something important there," I said. "Do we need to go find a tent somewhere and talk about it?"

"Yes. I think getting out of this heat would be wise," Iris replied as she fanned herself with her hand.

Minsheng appeared, hurrying after Nuri as the phoenix flew back and landed on my shoulder. He greeted them by name and then helped me usher them toward a tent. It appeared as if he'd been expecting them, and I tried not to get irritated that I'd not been told.

I followed him, however, falling in beside Iris at the back and watching their reactions and glances as they admired Sen and Roth, the Pegasus striding along beside Minsheng with the dryad on his back. Zephyr walked with me, his fingers entwined in mine, and I was pretty sure some of the organization members were confused.

*Maybe they don't know I can take human form*, he said.

*You'd think they'd have gotten the memo. We're not exactly hiding it anymore.*

*True, but everyone always expects me to be in dragon form.*

*You look sexier in human form.*

*I'd be worried if you thought otherwise.*

I grinned and fought back a chuckle as he squeezed my hand and we made our way into a small tent. The general was sitting at a desk near the back of it and looked up as we arrived.

Minsheng handled introductions again and made me wonder once more what was going on.

"It's good to finally meet you all. I've heard a lot about you and how you've aided Miss Carter so much already."

"Aella, please," I said, interrupting and letting them know I was still there. "And would someone like to fill me in?"

"Sorry," Minsheng replied. "You were sleeping when the organization called to say they'd managed to find something. And I had...other things on my mind at breakfast."

"We have been poring over some old texts for years in the hopes of finding something that once belonged to the four great elementals. With some help from the US army, we finally found this near the north pole." Iris beamed at me.

My mouth fell open. The north pole? The great elemental elves had left something near the north pole?

With a chuckle, one of the organization members stepped forward and unlocked the handcuffs on the bearer's wrist. Iris then came forward and put some numbers into the two combination locks on it. The fourth organization member then stepped forward to put their thumb on a small scanner revealed under that.

Finally, the briefcase opened to reveal a helmet. I could feel the power in it as soon as I stepped forward, and the four gemstones wrought into the top glowed.

"Henera," Iris said, beaming with pride. "This belongs to you."

# CHAPTER TWENTY

I stared at the helmet, standing in my private tent. I hadn't dared to take it out of the briefcase yet, and the organization thankfully hadn't made me. But I was going to have to do so soon.

It was powerful, and the organization must have spent a long time getting it for me as well as a lot of money. But I wasn't sure what it did. Did I want to put this on? Was it going to become stuck on me as the other four artifacts had?

*Only one way to find out,* Zephyr said.

*It's not you that's putting this thing on. What if it gets stuck on my head?*

*It's pretty, and it will hide your hair. You could not wash it for days, and no one would know.*

*I'd know. You'd know.*

*I wouldn't tell anyone.*

I rolled my eyes, but Zephyr was right. There was only one way I was going to find out what this did and how it worked. Neither the Sanctuary nor the organization knew what it could do. It wasn't something any of the great elves had ever worn in battle because it was designed by them for the Henera. It could only be wielded by someone who could control all four elements at once.

That fact alone had me worried. Worried that it would be putting me to the test the moment I put it on. Or it would get stuck.

Taking a deep breath, I picked it up anyway and brought it closer. The gemstones glowed, and I could feel a tingle in the air around the helmet.

I tried not to think about what could go wrong as I slipped it onto my head. At first, nothing happened and then there was a rush as my mind connected with the gemstones, each one feeling like a concentrated source of the element.

The helmet felt warm and almost alive, and it fit my head. Before I did anything with it, I lifted it to take it off. It came off easily.

*Looks like you'll have to keep washing your hair, after all,* Zephyr said, his chuckle making me grin.

*I'm good with that. I wouldn't want to end up with helmet hair.*

*I dunno; it would make getting it cut easy. You could have it trimmed to the same height as the helmet. And then no one would even know you had hair.*

*It would become a complete mess.*

*Not necessarily. You'd still be able to use your mind to neaten it.*

*I'm pretty sure that it's a waste of my energy to brush my hair with my powers.*

Zephyr exhaled as if he was pretending to be exasperated by my complaints, but I glanced his way and saw the merriment in his eyes. We were still on good terms. He wasn't upset about me getting yet another artifact.

Relieved that this helmet wasn't going to bind to me and wasn't going to cut my head off or do anything else that could make me scared to use it, I lifted it onto my head once more.

Yet again, I was wearing the helmet, and I had a tingling feeling in my mind. I reached toward the gemstones and felt the raw power. It was then that I realized the helmet was a lot like the tablets that the cult had taken. They felt as if they were storing magic in a similar way. It made me wonder if they could be used to power something.

*Probably worth talking to Minsheng,* Zephyr said. *He may have a better idea of what this can do and if we should do it.*

*Do you think he'll know when the organization doesn't?*

*He's studied those tablets and the portal and its pillars. If anyone has an idea if this is reacting the same way, he will.*

It was a good point. I took the helmet off once more and put it back in the box. Within a minute, I was carrying it over to the tent I hoped Minsheng would be in. He had been working with Chris, Daisy, and another couple of folks from Amcika on some tech and I hadn't seen him much, but he had made it clear that if I needed him for training, I could pull him away.

As soon as he noticed me, he came out of the tent, and we found somewhere secluded. I didn't want to show anyone what I had, so I quickly told him my theory in whispers and asked if he could help me check.

"I suspected something like this. Perhaps not exactly how the tablets work, but the gemstones in the helmet appear to have engravings and they're holding power. Let's go partway up the mountain and experiment," Minsheng replied as he reached into the backpack he had with him and pulled out the devices he had used on many occasions to monitor these sorts of things.

Grinning, I lifted us into the air and watched as Nuri and Roth took off as well. With Zephyr's help, we flew Minsheng along with us to the section of the mountain out of the way where we'd begun training in the last few days.

It wasn't entirely out of the way, and if anyone needed us from the camp, they could holler and we'd hear them, but it was far enough away we could converse quietly and try things while able to see a disturbance coming.

As soon as we had touched down and were ready to begin, I took the helmet out of the box and put it on my head. I was getting used to the strange tingling feeling it gave off and how it felt to connect to the gemstones. Unlike the tablets, they didn't appear to be trying to suck in my energy, but that could easily be because they felt so full of power.

When I had been wielding the tablets in battle, I had been aware of the strange way they wanted to be filled up. The way they'd wanted to stay connected to an elemental and drain them if they weren't full, but also how the pull and connection had become easier to resist as they'd grown fuller. A strange, living battery of elemental magic.

Of course, a lot of those had been broken in the battles, but we still had fragments and parts, some of which worked better than others. They weren't something I had chosen to use much in battle, especially lately, but I thought we needed to get them back out of storage and use them to fight off this dark elf.

For now, I had to see what I was wearing, however.

"Use them one element at a time," Minsheng said as he finished getting his devices ready. "They're giving off readings, but they mostly seem to be dormant."

I nodded, grateful that he was getting the same indication that I was.

After taking a deep breath, I reached for the gemstones with my mind. I could feel a thin connection there to each of them as if it came from the stones themselves, but I made it stronger and explored them deeper. I wanted to be sure I wasn't doing something troubling before I did it.

As I connected more to the white one, the gemstone feeling full of air power and the element itself, it felt like an easy and gentle hand holding my mind. This gemstone wasn't hungry. I then reached out to the air around me and drew on the crystal as I moved the air around.

"Wow," Minsheng said, and he pressed buttons and turned knobs on the device. "You're right that this is like the tablets. But it's also different. The whole thing is...gentler. More harmonious. And it's using very little energy."

Blinking, I processed what that meant. In truth, I could feel it. Using the gemstones was almost effortless. I played with the air, swirling it around, beginning to make a tornado and then letting it go again.

Once I had played with the air for a while, I chose the next element and reached into the rocks and plants around me. I was quickly moving them as well, the control feeling effortless and easier than normal.

Over the next few minutes, I tried them all. The

gemstones supplied energy as well and made everything easier, as if I'd mastered all of the elements and how they could be used. As if I'd practiced with all four for years.

"That's one powerful helmet," Minsheng said when we were done. "And it seems almost entirely due to those four gemstones."

"I'll take care of the thing then and wear it into battle, I guess. Although I'm wary about what it will do if I am connected to it for too long and I drain the gemstones too far."

"I can understand the concern, but if it's anything like the tablets, then you'll get some warning. Just be careful not to drain them while not in battle."

Given I was thinking about spending the next few minutes seeing if I could fill them up, I nodded and sat down. Minsheng sat nearby, under the shade of a tree. Zephyr encouraged Sen, Roth, and Nuri to join him in practicing to work together and being prepared for all sorts of scenarios.

I marveled at the cooperation and skill around me. Over the years since I'd found Zephyr, we had come a long way. It seemed our journey wasn't over, however. While I was adorned with objects that aided me in my bonds to my mythicals, I was now wearing something that could make me a lot stronger.

Concentrating again, I pushed my way deeper in connection with the air crystal and then sent some energy to it in a similar way to the tablets. Although the tablets sucked at the energy greedily, the gemstone didn't. At least not in the same way. It accepted it, seeming to present itself as an empty vessel ready to fill and store it, but it wasn't hungry for it, and it didn't feel as if I had to struggle to resist the pull.

Aware that it was unlikely to be different with the other gemstones, I didn't add anything to them for now. I favored using air in battle, using it to fly, push objects and enemies around, and speed up my reflexes.

I continued to fill the air crystal, noticing that it also took however much I put in without getting choked up. It was like a bottomless pit, and it made me wonder just how much energy the greats must have put into it.

Before I drained myself, I stopped and asked Minsheng to come over.

"Can you measure how much energy these things have in them? Like the display of a cell and how much juice is remaining in the battery? I want to know what difference I'm making and if we can find a way to work out what's already in these things."

Minsheng looked thoughtful and tilted his head to the side.

"I might be able to do that. I'd need to study them a lot more. Take a lot more readings and work out how much is added and where it stores it. But I think I can do that over time. Have you put more in now?"

I nodded and considered taking the helmet off, but Minsheng pulled out another device and scanned the gemstones while it was still on my head.

"I'll have a chat to some of the other scientists about them, but I think if we get you to add or take away and we keep getting readings at different points, we'll be able to work out a rough indicator."

It was a good enough offering, and it made me feel

happier. The organization had found me something that should help in battles and life in general. With something like this, I could dump any energy I had at the end of a day I wasn't fighting, and it would be there for me when I needed it another day.

A battery for my powers. That would be hugely beneficial.

I was about to suggest I put more in when there was a loud shout from the camp. It was followed swiftly by another one from up on top of the mountain and another by the tunnels.

"An attack," Minsheng said as I got to my feet. "Protect the entrance above and then come down and help."

"What about you?"

*I'll fly him where he's needed*, Roth said as he hurried over to my Shishou's side. *We can't all help on the top.*

*Sen and Nuri help in cavern.*

I wasn't going to waste time arguing and simply nodded as Sen jumped onto Nuri's back and Minsheng climbed onto Roth's. Zephyr took my hand as we powered into the air, beside each other in elven form.

The top of the mountain always seemed a long way off, but we could fly fast, the pair of us so practiced that we moved with ease. Above us, I could make out two of the earth elves from Amcika, and I was grateful that they were there and standing with their hands on the rubble.

With the practice we'd been doing at working with other elves to meld control, I hoped it would give us the collective power we needed to beat back whatever force was trying to push through.

Less than a minute after we'd begun flying, we had

landed on the small flat area outside the mountain and we hurried over to the other elves. The relief on their faces at seeing Zephyr and me there was replaced by curiosity as they saw the helmet fitted to my head.

"Long story," I said, "But it should help us. How many are there?"

"Can't tell, but they're packing a punch, and they added in more pressure when we resisted them," one said, his breathing labored.

I nodded and reached with my mind through the small air gap we'd left, trying to find the bodies within. Zephyr lent his mind to the cause and connected with the elements with the other earth elementals. He took up some of the strain, and their hope returned.

Pretty sure the three of them could hold for a while and leave me free to act independently, I reached through the air, finding the first twenty dark earth elves waiting on the other side. But then my mind continued past what remained of the extra wall I'd created and found another squad of ten. And then another, each one waiting.

Forty earth elves against the four of us. This was going to be a challenge.

# CHAPTER TWENTY-ONE

Trying not to panic, I took control of the air and felt for the earth as well. I boxed the elves in, stealing their oxygen and pulling it out while Zephyr was in human form. There wasn't going to be time for him to take dragon form and exhale into the tunnel again while also keeping the tunnel from being opened outward, but there were other ways to make this work.

I fought to keep an air barrier in place as a squad of ten air elves appeared as well. Whoever was directing this bunch of dark elves was learning our tactics. But I'd gotten stronger. A lot stronger.

Using the air and earth stones, I worked with my allies and held firm against the dark elves using air. It was still hard, even with the boost I had. The forty elves were working well together, and we were still new to the process. I didn't know how to make the most of the power in the gemstones either.

It took forever for the elves inside the tunnel to show signs of running out of oxygen, and I felt awful as they weakened. The relief on our control was almost immediate, however. I was grateful when Zephyr felt he could let go, morph into dragon form, and exhale a cloud of gas into the tunnel.

The air elves grew furious at this development, and they assaulted the air barrier I'd created with so much force I had to step back.

Not needing to fight the control of the dark elves, there was nothing the earth elementals could do but strengthen the blockage to the tunnel again and repair what damage the elves had done.

I held up under the fight from the air elves as best I could, aware that the ten dark elves who were pushing me were stronger than any of the earth elves. They'd decided to make up in strength what they didn't have in numbers in this case.

Despite that, I held, for now, closing my eyes and focusing on my best element. I pushed back and held firm, making the most of the gemstones' power to keep me going as I then reached farther out and around the air elves. Without them seeming to realize it, I put an air barrier up behind them and then let the first one go.

At the same time, I quickly grabbed control of the paralyzing vapor Zephyr controlled and hit them with it as swiftly as I could. Within a minute, fifty dark elves were lying out cold, and I could finally relax.

Panting, I stepped back and looked at the others with me.

"It's done. If you two could stay up here and keep an eye out for whatever they might try next, that would be useful, but Zephyr and I should return to the main entrance. The dark elves are pushing on every front."

"Go, we've got this, Henera." The nearest earth elf saluted me, and it made me blink in surprise before Zephyr let out a roar and flew into the air. The powerful downbeat almost blasted both earth elves off their feet with displaced air, but they grinned.

I returned the gesture before I powered into the sky as well and hurried after Zephyr to land on his back and let him carry me to the valley below.

The whole area seemed deathly quiet, the fighting happening inside the mountain and the tunnel. On the way down, I connected with Sen and then Roth to see what they were facing.

The soldiers had bolstered the defense inside the mountain and they were holding on for now, but the sea tunnel was being pushed hard by water and earth elementals trying to get out. I was also pretty sure some fire elementals must be involved, the heat there almost unbearable.

Zephyr picked up on what I saw and headed for the tunnel so we could wade in there as well.

As we got near the ground, I blasted off Zephyr's back, so I could get into the fight sooner. It meant I was ahead of him as he landed. The heat wall by the tunnel entrance was intense, and there was a fire elf nearby. Although I could make things cooler or hotter with air, it took a long time to do anything significant. Someone nearby was heating the area with efficiency only a fire elf could achieve.

I hurried into the tunnel where the fighting was

happening. The sea was behind Roth, Cherisse, and several other elves, along with Minsheng, Gwaelon, and Ruehnar.

Falling in beside Roth and Gwaelon, I reached for the seawater at the back of the cave with my mind and prepared to defend myself or preemptively strike. As it was, it was a short respite as I was hit with hot, salty water from one side before I'd finished getting close enough. I rocked back, Roth coming to my defense and blocking it with his body.

Worried about the heat levels and that Roth might burn, I reached out with my mind to take control of the air and do my best to block the spray and send it back. At the same time, I looked for the source of the water to neutralize it, or at the very least, the fire being used to make it burn hot.

I tried not to panic when my mind came up against either a large water creature or a group of water elves working together so effectively that they were like an immovable force.

*There's something powerful up ahead*, Roth confirmed.

Frowning, I used the air to reach forward and work out what it was. Something needed to be done to stop them, and I was the only one with enough reach.

Zephyr appeared beside me in human form. Although he preferred the earth element, his mind joined mine, probing forward and feeling for whatever lay ahead.

There were some dark elves near us, but they were drawing the water out of the earth and tunneling around them and feeding it back into whatever water elemental was creating this gush of water.

I took another step forward, blasting a couple of dark

elves off their feet as Gwaelon gathered some of the hotter water to him as well.

*The walls and roof are getting dangerous*, Zephyr pointed out a moment later, his mind leaving the space near mine as he patched it up.

Continuing, I found the source of the hot water. What appeared to be twins, almost identical-feeling elves stood together hand in hand. Around them, the tunnel steamed and the water at their feet churned with heat.

I wasn't sure what to do. I hadn't expected such an obvious combination, nor for there to be only two of them. What was so special about these two elves, and why were they so hard to challenge mentally?

Although my strength lay most in my range, I was used to being mentally stronger than most elves as well. But these two were on another level again. I'd never felt anything like it.

*We need some more earth elves in here to keep the tunnel safe, and then I can focus on helping you.*

*Sen send help*, she replied before I could think of a suitable solution.

After sending a wave of affection her way, I monitored the twin dark elves I couldn't see with anything but my abilities and couldn't yet challenge either way. They were concentrating on their task and I wasn't sure they knew I was there beyond the few attempts I had made to wrestle control away from them.

With no other fire elves in the tunnel with me, I wasn't sure I could challenge the fire twin, but I might be able to overwhelm the other with a water elemental or two to help.

Not sure who to ask when there were so many fighting the water being jetted in our direction and melding it with the cooler seawater from behind, I hesitated. This had been a well-thought-out attack, but there was always a way to beat the enemy. It just had to be found.

I tried not to panic when over five minutes later, I hadn't managed to get any further toward defeating them. This was a battle, and in battles, a person couldn't sit around and wait for the chance to make a winning strike.

Thankfully, more earth elves showed up, and Zephyr soon had them fixing some of the difficult and dangerous parts of the tunnel, making sure the fight we were going to have wasn't going to bring the tunnel down on us.

It meant he could join me again and we stepped forward, Roth coming as well to protect us from water blasts so we could focus. I took Zephyr's hand and then held my other arm out, hoping that one of the other water elves would get the idea and help.

Gwaelon was still nearby and came up to grab my hand. To my surprise, Cherisse fell in on the other side of him. Their minds reached out to merge with mine. It was strange, after all the time being enemies to have something in common to fight for.

Knowing it wasn't the first time I'd turned a group of enemies into allies, I concentrated on what we needed to do, merging my control with theirs. Once we were combining our efforts, I took the entire group forward, aiming for the female dark elf. I was terrified to attack one of the pair, but I wasn't alone this time.

Picking a section of water that was about to be jetted out at us from the steamy area, I encouraged my group to hit it hard. At first, nothing happened, the elf was so strong and some of the elements were moving so fast it would have been difficult to take control under normal circumstances.

With the water spraying everywhere, it was hard to tell what was happening. I didn't feel too much resistance, but that didn't mean that we had succeeded and the elf was defeated. It could mean they were in trouble for another reason. That perhaps they were running out of power, but I wasn't going to count on the latter.

Eventually, I felt the resistance that meant we couldn't get any farther or take control, the pushback of a mind holding elements in good condition and not pushing harder than they had to.

This was feeling as if it was a hopeless cause. I couldn't find a way to get past these two elves, and Roth had to block an attack once more, the sting he felt when the boiling hot water hit him making me wince as well.

These two elves were a problem.

Of course, they would run out of stamina eventually, but I was pretty sure the elves with me were also growing tired. On top of that, these were just two of the dark elves ahead.

As another couple of elves appeared and aided the fight, Ruehnar gave us his mind as well, melding in until we were five strong.

With Roth creating a distraction by jetting some of the water back from the center of his head the five of us tried again. We reached out and seized control of the water, challenging whoever was there. This time when we hit the control of another elf the elements became ours. Several of the elves stepped back as if they'd been slapped or shoved.

The water elf of the twins fought back and resisted, however, her body moving as she took a different stance to fight us with her mind. Almost subconsciously, I mimicked the movement, putting my limbs in the same outward position and squaring myself off to her despite only being able to feel her presence with the air I controlled.

Zephyr copied as well, seeming to sense what I was doing, and then I noticed Gwaelon shrug and do the same before the others joined in. Pushing ahead with our minds, I finally felt her snap and the control of the elements came to us.

She let out a furious scream, the sound part roar of defiance and cry of outrage at being thwarted, and then her mind attacked back. I noticed the twin with her wince and it was as if his fire faltered for a few seconds.

I took control of that as well, cooling down the area so it was no longer baking us.

With everything briefly under the control of the five of us, we held our ground while the rest of the elves with us hurried forward, carrying tranquilizer rifles the military had supplied and various other assorted weapons.

Although I'd tried to convince the Amcika elves to fight back in a more peaceful manner, they weren't all in agreement, and Cherisse still technically called the shots with her cult of elves.

I tried not to think about the senseless violence and instead focused on holding onto the elements and knocking out as many of the elves as possible. Several dark elves went down within seconds, and it finally gave us the advantage in the battle.

The twins soon recovered, however, everyone else working hard to protect them and block attacks meant for them. They worked together, despite controlling different elements. It was a puzzling new development, but it made me want to capture them alive if I could and talk to them.

They hit me hard with everything they had, however, trying to take back the fire and water at the same time. While I had help with the water, I didn't have any help with the fire until Zephyr slipped his mind in with mine, the more practiced of anyone at adapting to me.

I thought we would fail to hold them back, and I shifted to see if I could get a shot on one of them while they were distracted and the other elves were taking care of the rest of our adversaries.

It meant I also had my attention divided, but I hung on as long as I could and lifted my rifle. I hit the guy, trying to ease the pressure on my mind. At the same time, a couple more soldiers rushed up and joined us. They quickly crouched behind Roth and near me. They helped take out the two dark elves, so many darts hitting them that they soon went down.

"I want them alive and somewhere I can talk to them when they wake up," I said to the nearest soldier, knowing of everyone near me that they would see my orders carried out and make sure the major knew I'd given them.

"I'd like much the same," Gwaelon replied, and I was pretty sure Cherisse nodded along with him.

After acknowledging their words I backed off, feeling the area calm as the elves around me pushed forward.

Confident that everyone here could hold the line, that left one more place for us to check in on and make sure was covered.

Cherisse came with me, and it made me realize how after telling me that she didn't care about the exits that both times we'd had fights, she'd ended up at the tunnel to the sea.

"I'm a water elf. It was where I could help best. And Simon made a good point about us needing to watch our backs and make sure that they couldn't attack us from behind while we were trying to get back in," she explained when I raised an eyebrow.

"Good enough reason."

"I'm not entirely heartless either, you know."

"I never said you were. I may not agree with you on a lot of things, including opening the portals, but I have a certain level of respect for the ability of yourself and your elves in a fight. I'm glad to be your ally now, even if we weren't in the past."

"That makes two of us, Henera. Now, let's make sure those scum don't take the rest of my mountain." She grinned as she finished speaking, and I found myself letting out a small laugh as Zephyr chuckled.

It was time to get to the big fight and help push back another wave.

## CHAPTER TWENTY-TWO

It didn't take long to see that the elves inside the mountain and main cavern room were struggling. The dark elves were more numerous than before. As they had done at the other two battle areas, they had improved their tactics and strategy to the point that the cult, Sanctuary elves, and the soldiers were hard-pressed to simply hold the line.

Once more I waded into battle, helping the nearest elves regain their footing, turning the tide of lots of small battles with blasts of air while Zephyr shook small areas of ground and shifted rock to swallow limbs. I was getting closer to Sen and Nuri as I moved toward the elevator shaft. I couldn't see Simon or Sen yet. Nuri was flying high and shooting well-aimed firebolts from his mouth on very specific targets.

I was worried about the level of violence, but I also needed to stop being so cautious and let go of it. I was struggling to adapt and change.

By the time I got close enough to the elevator to see what was going on, Cherisse had gone off to one side to defend the stairwell entrance. I was beginning to tire. There were so many elves that it was sometimes hard to move in any direction.

Zephyr kept close to me, one of his hands entwined in mine and our heads moving more than the rest of us. Magic was now so natural we only needed to look the right way and focus. After blasting a larger group of air elves back, I challenged some of them for control, finding they were weak enough I could take on four of them alone.

A stronger set of minds hit me, however. Zephyr rushed to join my focus, his mind rescuing me and the stabbing pain they'd created in the center of my forehead.

*Use the helmet to hang on,* Zephyr said. *I know they'll be getting tired, and I can see Simon gathering some elves to push back.*

I did as he suggested, trusting his assessment of the battle while I fought on. It was easy to use the helmet gemstones and pull power out of them. Within seconds it had allowed me to not only beat the elves back but take more air and blast some off their feet and pin them down long enough for soldiers or cult elves to take them out of the equation.

Moving closer, I followed Zephyr and looked for the next fight I could help with. It didn't take long. Around the base of the elevator, several very strong-looking elves had managed to create a barrier and were protected behind it, controlling the elevator shaft and the air in it.

I noticed that there was another dark elf similar to the twins, who was wearing different clothes as they had been. While there was something almost mindlessly soldier-like about the majority of the dark elves, these particular elves had more of a mind of their own. They were more expressive, more targeted, and a lot stronger.

My eyes locked with the air elf as my mind came into contact with the barrier he had created. I stepped into the space beside Simon, feeling Zephyr step up the other side.

"Good to see you, Henera," Simon said, also staring at the air elf. "Shall I introduce you to the latest air elf who thinks they have what it takes to challenge you?"

I let out a cross between a snort and a laugh, surprised by the snark in Simon's voice.

*Got what it takes to challenge you? Please. They've not got the hair to look amazing flying the way you do,* Zephyr added, and I chuckled again.

*No one looks as good as you do flying, don't worry,* I replied to him.

*Of course, they don't. No one else is a dragon. I'm the biggest badass in the skies. In more ways than one. Have you seen the size of me? Not even Batman casts a shadow like I do.*

My chuckle turned into a laugh as elves and soldiers stared at me. The dark elf general we were facing off against reacted.

*They don't understand how funny you are. Shall we show them how serious we are instead?*

*Gladly,* he replied as we merged our control.

Several other air elves did the same. One of them was Simon. Grateful for the support, I moved straight for the barrier and snatched the elements in it from the dark elf.

At first, he smirked, not pushed hard, but I increased the pressure. Zephyr and some of the others did the same. I didn't stop staring at him, making sure he could see the determined look on my face and understand I was focused entirely on him.

The smile faltered a moment, and the mirth disappeared from his eyes, but I could see him trying to pretend it was still easy. Another mind joined with us, adding to the pressure. Still, he didn't give.

Not sure how tired the elves with me were, I reached into the gemstone in the helmet once more and pulled out more energy. The dark elf took a step back, his eyes going wide, and the corner of my mouth lifted.

*Just a little more*, Zephyr said, but before he'd finished speaking, the dark elf called something in a language I didn't understand. Several more elves rushed to his side, and the resistance to our attack grew again.

"Need more air elves over here," I called, aware there were still plenty who weren't working with us yet.

His elves responded more swiftly, but I wasn't going to be beaten easily. More minds joined mine, at least ten. It was the largest number of minds I'd merged with and it felt strange, but I set my jaw and focused with everything I had. I was breaking through this barrier.

At first, I thought I was mistaken, but then something gave, and the elf reeled backward. Soldiers opened fire, taking advantage of the lack of resistance. Over half the dark elves on the other side went down and the elves with me rushed forward, using their abilities and weapons to overwhelm the rest.

Before I could stop him, the dark air elf pushed up to his feet, grabbed some more air he controlled, and solidified it around him. He darted for the elevator shaft more swiftly than I could have believed possible and was gone as I grabbed the air.

*We'll get him next time*, Zephyr said as he blasted a fire elf who was about to attack a group of unsuspecting earth elves. They were trying to corner a group of Sanctuary elves and it made me feel better to see the two groups working together and keeping each other safe. At least in battle, they could respect each other.

I wanted to go after the air elf, but I heard shouts from behind, and Nuri rushed over my head in that direction.

As I turned, I saw Cherisse get hit with a large boulder, her body going flying. I reached into the air, pushing back on the boulder and slowing her down as gently as I could while making sure she didn't hit the ground as I ran to her.

She was out cold and going to be in a world of pain. One of her arms was bent at a strange angle. Other elves came running up as I reached into her body with my mind. I could feel the blood near her stomach pooling where it shouldn't be and took control of it.

Although I wasn't sure what I was doing, I had the power to keep her alive longer and hoped a medic elf with more experience could do the rest. A soldier got to me first as Zephyr yelled for a medic as well and threw an air barrier around us to ensure it didn't get any worse.

As the soldier pulled out medication from a bag and I explained the internal bleeding I could feel, an elf I recognized finally got there. The medic I'd helped several times came through the barrier as Zephyr let them in and then closed it again with him on the outside.

The medic knelt beside me, and her control merged

with mine. It was a relief, and I let her take over, guiding me and the extra power I offered her. Slowly we fixed Cherisse on the inside while I stopped it from getting any worse.

I wasn't sure exactly what was happening, and I think the medic was trying things and hoping it worked. We kept Cherisse breathing and her heart kept beating, however.

With no idea how much time was passing, I frequently drew on the water, earth, and air gemstones to help power the healing and make sure that the medic didn't run out of her ability.

"It's not perfect. But it will keep her alive until we can get a better person on it and get her under the tech so I can see better detail."

"When it comes to finishing the job, if you need my power, let me know. I'll come help," I said as I got up and let the rest of the medical team take over.

"Thank you, Henera. I'm sure it will mean a lot to Cherisse to know you gave so much to save her and were still willing to give more."

I blinked, not having thought about it like that. To me, life was precious. Cherisse was an ally. Someone I was fighting beside and risking my life beside. No one deserved to die defending their home and the people living in it from evil.

Before I could say anything or begin to explain my thoughts, the soldiers had Cherisse on a stretcher and were carrying her away, and the medic was called to aid the next person.

*Time to get back to the fight*, Zephyr said, pulling me back to the present.

I nodded and reached into the boulder they'd thrown at

Cherisse. It looked as if it was made from the rock of the mountain, and it made me wonder what they'd pulled apart to construct it before I looked for my next target.

As there had been a fire, water, and air elf with strong command of their elements, there was also a strong-looking earth elf, throwing rocks around and making walls and floors shake and ripple.

Without hesitation, I threw the boulder at him, gripping the air along the way and making sure it flew straight and true until it smacked into the elf and knocked him off his feet. He never saw it coming, and it pounded him into the floor. The boulder kept going, knocking several other dark elves off their feet.

Heads turned and looked at me, the Sanctuary elves with wide eyes, but the cult elves cheered and whooped with delight, especially the ones who had witnessed the same boulder knock their leader off her feet and shatter her body.

The dark elf didn't move either, and I considered stopping the companions who went to him from doing so. Instead, I relented, letting them take his broken body back to the stairwell. As he disappeared into the dark, carried by another earth elf, I wondered what they would do with him. They didn't appear to be as compassionate nor trying to save him, but they were carrying him away as if he was important.

With the powerful elf taken care of and Simon coming over to help direct the fight in Cherisse's absence, the rest of the dark elves finally pulled back, retreating up the stairs for a second time.

I exhaled as I finally stopped flinging magic around and

let my control of everything but the small air barrier around me go. My reserves weren't entirely depleted, but I could see many exhausted elves around me, and I had drawn a phenomenal amount of power out of the helmet I wore. Far more than I could ever hope to put in during a week.

This fight had been won by luck and good strategy and a helmet that had been gifted to me from millennia ago and recovered by the organization. This battle shouldn't have been won at all.

Painful in places I hadn't realized I'd been hurt or used, I walked slowly toward the group of gathering leaders outside the main entrance. Many of them looked just as tired, but none of them were relaxed either. There was still a lot of aftercare and cleanup to do. I was sure that there was going to be a discussion.

Whoever was in charge of the dark elves in the mountain had grown stronger while we had simply waited and guarded a perimeter. We had barely won. And that meant one very big thing. We couldn't afford to wait for them to bring more people in through the portal and get stronger.

"I want a meeting with everyone important in an hour," I said to them as I walked up. "Get as many elves and soldiers as possible resting and eating, and then we have a lot to talk about."

Minsheng smiled as he nodded, and the major threw me a salute. I wasn't sure Simon looked as pleased, but Ronan and Sierrathen bowed, and Iris looked as if she was proud of me when I started walking away and she joined the others, having heard what I'd said.

*We should rest as well until then,* Zephyr said, picking up

Sen and cuddling the exhausted myconid to him. I nodded, then looked over the four mythicals I was bonded with.

*Food and rest for us too. We need it.*

Without another word, we made our way to the main, canteen-style tent. I was pretty sure it would be incredibly unkind of us to command anyone to fetch us food and half-expected there not to be anything ready in the kitchens to feed this many people. Thankfully, I was wrong.

Some of the elves who had been dismissed from battle or had finished defending an area and hadn't been able to get close to fight had come here. The smell was heavenly and I was soon sitting down with many other elves and tucking in.

We'd survived another battle, but all we'd done was defend a line. And we'd lost Cherisse, at least for a while.

# CHAPTER TWENTY-THREE

Before I went to find everyone to discuss our response to the attack, I made my way to the medical tent to check on Cherisse. I'd offered to help heal her if I could, and I intended to keep that promise.

The tent had been set up with medical equipment, some of it strange and from the mountain and of mythical origin and some of it as if it was out of any medical facilities in the human world.

After the battle, it was a hum of activity. I drowned it out and focused on finding Cherisse among the most injured. It didn't take me long to spot her on a raised bed, the medic and several other elves standing around her holding different bits of tech.

I went to her side as quickly as I could, trying not to distract the medics helping to repair her body.

She looked better than she had, the elven healing capabilities no doubt helping her body repair damage as well as the elves around her. I reached out with my mind to gently feel for what might be going on and found one person working to help Cherisse, the elf not holding a device beside her bed.

As our minds briefly touched, she noticed me and looked up.

"How is she?" I asked. "And do you need any help?"

"She's not completely okay yet, but we're getting there. I've been told that you helped her in the battle."

Nodding, I moved closer, the other men and women around her making space for me.

I listened as they discussed what would be needed to heal Cherisse and where the damage was done. It was clear that they had tried to repair the damage in a few areas and not succeeded as well as they'd have wanted to.

"Can I help? I still have energy left after the battle, and I can merge my control with any of you that need it, probably even all of you at once. I want to see her on her feet again."

They turned to stare at me as I spoke, but none of them appeared aggressive or hesitant. One of them stared open-mouthed.

"You'd really help?" the nearest male elf asked.

"Yes. She's your leader, and she's a strong elf who is doing what she thinks is best for her followers. I might not agree with her or her methods, but I respect life and her desire to try to make this world a better place for mythicals."

This pacified their surprise, and the female elf opposite me took charge. She spent another few minutes running through a list of body parts that needed fixing and how to do so, everyone else seeming to understand. I followed as much of it as I could, wanting to make sure I was helping and would be able to respond with the other elves.

When she'd finished explaining, she looked at me.

"If we reach out to the parts of Cherisse we need to control, can you add your power and help make it happen?"

I nodded, hoping I could and pretty sure that I was going to need to if Cherisse was going to live. Zephyr stood beside me and slipped his hand into mine.

"I can help as well," he said aloud, although his gaze was on me.

I saw the light in his eyes and the strange hope in them. He'd been feeling awful since he'd broken the pillars to save me. This was a chance to save someone we should hate. A chance to use our desire to see no one else harmed in a good way. In a lot of ways, it felt like redemption.

All of us would live to put right what had happened together. And defend this mountain once more.

We reached out with our minds. Zephyr and I melded together so naturally, it was almost like breathing now. It had helped that we'd practiced and could do so easily, but I strongly suspected it also helped that he was essentially using my abilities. The power had the same source anyway.

The other elves were reaching out and connecting where they were needed, so I followed their example and gently added my control to theirs. I tried not to direct anything, simply adding my power and letting the others guide me.

It wasn't easy when we were dealing with four elements, and the elves we were with only had to focus on one each, but we were spread across multiple locations.

Over the next few minutes, the elf in charge started directing us to move between the organs and body parts, fixing in an order that didn't make sense at first. As more time went on, however, and I saw how some elements interacted with others, I realized that this was as complicated an operation as a traditional human surgeon in a hospital. Although this was being done by magic and without needing to cut anyone open.

During the process, I could only let my powers be drained and hope that I didn't do anything too crazy by accident, especially as I was used to the more brutal acts of war and fighting with strength and force. Using my abilities delicately was something I wasn't very practiced at.

Time slipped by in a blur as the elves worked, and I did my best to follow their lead and heal Cherisse. Soon I could start to see the difference in her appearance. Before she had been deathly pale, but color was returning to her features. Her breathing also grew gentler and deeper.

It was wonderful to be part of something so amazing, and it gave me hope that elves could become a hugely beneficial part of society. If this was one of the ways we could help people, what could it save? Would it mean that cancer was no longer a problem?

Of course, there was a flaw in my idea. There were only so many elves and not enough to be a doctor or surgeon who healed and took over every single operation that must be performed each day. But to save lives that might otherwise be lost would be phenomenal.

Finally, we were working on the last element of the damage, broken bones that needed to be mended more for comfort and to hasten recovery time than because she couldn't continue living.

It was strange to relax as the job was complete and realize how tense I'd become. I had aches in my body where I had been tense and stood for too long, but Zephyr's fingers were still entwined in mine, and he gave me a gentle squeeze.

"There," the elf in charge said as she smiled. "I think that should do the trick. Thank you, everyone."

There were more smiles and nods as a nurse-like elf came over and started checking the basic health of Cherisse.

I didn't know what I'd expected, but Cherisse hadn't woken up. Her body was fine, but she was still out cold. If the others had been concerned, I'd have been more worried, but the other elves moved away and on to the next elf who needed healing and help while leaving me there to stand by Cherisse.

"She'll wake up when her mind has also had a chance to recover," Simon's voice said from beside me. "Even with our capabilities, something like this is traumatic for the person who goes through it. The mind has to process it and check everything is working well enough to wake her. It's a good thing in a lot of ways."

"Then we should plan how to push these elves back, so she's got something to wake up for," I said, hearing the conviction in my voice and being as surprised by it as Simon was.

I tried not to worry about the other injured and sick elves in the tent as I made my way out, my hand still in Zephyr's and the rest of my mythicals going with me.

Simon didn't follow, and I glanced back before leaving to see him standing by her side, his mouth moving in words meant only for her. Giving him some privacy, I made my way to the small command tent. I was going to be early for our meeting, but I had nowhere else to go, and I didn't want to give the enemy any more opportunity to rally and prepare for another attack.

The camp was mostly quiet now, a lot of elves resting and recovering their strength. It felt eerie, but it was for the best. We needed to recover.

I found Minsheng, Ronan, Daisy, and the general inside the tent. They looked up and smiled at me before I realized they were on a video call. They ushered me forward as Zephyr held the tent flap open for Roth, Nuri, and Sen to also come through.

As I came around to see who they were talking to, I noticed that Minsheng was holding several devices and studying something with them.

"As you can see, the strange behavior here is happening in relation to the activity where you are too," the President said, his voice coming to me before I saw him.

I gave him a slight wave but didn't speak as I sat down on a stool beside Minsheng. I finally took the helmet I was wearing off, realizing for the first time since the battle that I was still wearing it, and I looked awful. At some point, I had gotten covered in a thin layer of dirt that then streaked with sweat.

As I took the helmet off the difference in the skin underneath it made it more obvious I was filthy.

"Normally a soldier would be reprimanded for appearing in front of me looking so disheveled," the President said. "But I have never entirely understood that. It's clear you've not rested properly after the battle to come in here as you are. You should take care of yourself as well, Aella-Faye."

"I've eaten, and I'm sitting now," I replied. "Tell me what's going on at your end."

"From what Minsheng is telling me, I believe the dark elf is trying to attack here and weaken us whenever an attack isn't in progress where you are."

I lifted my eyebrows and looked between Minsheng and the video screen.

"I'm getting the same signature coming through the Texas portal, through the video call," my Shishou explained as he held up the devices.

"You're getting an attack now?" I asked.

"We are. It's not awful to cope with, please don't be concerned. We can pull back enough from the portal that there's little the elf can do. And we've increased the defenses farther out."

"Good. The dark elves here have been putting some of their best magic users to the task of getting out of the mountain. I'm sure they'll try to take the Texas portal if they succeed."

There was a silence as I finished speaking. It was clear I'd said something they feared but no one had dared utter.

"Okay, I understand you're about to plan how to take back the mountain there. Know you have my full support to use the resources at your disposal. Our team here is still working with the Mexican government to make sure that we have as much of their cooperation and aid as possible."

I saw the general's hands ball into fists at these words,

bothered by this. It made me wonder if the Mexicans were being difficult deliberately, but if that was true, there was little I could do about it. I'd work with whatever I had and leave politics to the politicians and be grateful I wasn't involved for once.

"We'll let you know our plans as soon as we've formed them," the general replied, and the President ended the call.

No one spoke or moved, and I could feel a weight in the room. We were up against a lot, and I had no sure idea how we were going to take and hold the mountain in the long term. Not without considerable resources.

"Minsheng, can you measure the gemstones in the helmet again?" I said when he began turning off the devices. "I'd like to have an idea of what I've got left in them if possible."

"Hmmm. That would help in working out their full capacity too." He took the helmet off me, and I got up again and went over to the small structure of the mountain that formed a battle map for us to plan with.

"It's clear they're bringing more dark elves through the portal and building their forces inside the mountain," Ronan said as he came to stand beside me.

With Zephyr on my other side and Sen bounding up to perch on the edge of the table, we must make a strange sight, but it wasn't long before the others joined us.

"They'll bring more through and make our task harder," I added when I had the attention of everyone in the tent.

"Agreed," Simon said as he swept the tent opening aside and came inside, the major and Sierrathen with him.

They walked up to the other side of the table and made it clear that this meeting had begun with everyone we had available. I hoped that Cherisse agreed with whatever we chose to do.

*She's alive to see what we choose because of you. I know she'll understand.*

*I hope so because I'm starting to fear that her mountain can't be saved. At least not with a portal in it.*

*That's probably true.*

"Okay," I said, bringing everyone's attention back to me. "Let's go over what we do know and what we've got. Then we can work out the best course of action and if we need to beg for any more resources from anyone."

There was a slight chuckle from the general, and Ronan smiled at my last sentence before everyone started listing off how many fighters they had and what types. Minsheng and Daisy made notes and tokens were added to the 3D map in front of us to represent each group and what they specialized in.

I noticed a dragon appeared along with smaller tokens for each of the mythicals and me. Someone had added a small paper helmet to a female figure, and it made me smile to see it. At least somebody was having fun with this. I could appreciate the humorous attention to detail.

Minutes and hours ticked by as we talked, working out what we were up against as best we could and what we were going to need to attack.

We were interrupted once, an elf coming to me to inform us that the few dark elves we'd captured alive, including the twins who had tried to break out of the earth tunnel, had escaped.

I swore, knowing that they would have been invaluable to provide information on what we were up against, and worried about what they might have learned and could give back to the enemy. It made our attack more pressing.

After checking no one was majorly hurt and finding that they'd gotten away by sneaking past the stairwell guards after setting a fire in the main cavern, I brought the focus back to the discussion at hand. How were we going to secure the portal again, and what forces were we going to use to do it?

# CHAPTER TWENTY-FOUR

"No. That won't work either." Sierrathen sighed as she pointed at a group of dark elves that hadn't been taken into account and could come around and attack a key set of soldiers from behind.

I exhaled, trying not to get too frustrated at yet another plan being shot down.

"It's no good," I said. "I'm going to have to be a distraction and go to the portal. I've got to draw everyone in toward it and fight whatever is there when I get there."

"You and your mythicals can't do that alone," Simon replied, his eyes going wider.

"Do you have a better idea?" I asked, noticing he had been very quiet and hadn't offered much of anything in the way of solutions.

"When you're talking about collapsing the entire mountain while Cherisse isn't here to tell you otherwise, of course I want to have a better idea. Anything that doesn't collapse the mountain in on itself is a better idea."

I frowned, knowing this was likely to be a sticking

point that didn't go away. It was something that was going to be a problem. If I couldn't get Simon to accept it, I was never going to get Cherisse to understand.

"I don't want to collapse the mountain," I said as I thought of a way to explain it that Simon would understand. "I know it's home to a lot of people, and I know they deserve to have it preserved. But we can't hold an open portal like this. There aren't enough elves to stand up against the dark elf. Not for a prolonged period of time."

"We don't agree on that," Simon replied.

"You should," Cherisse said as she strode into the room.

Everyone turned to her as she walked over to the table. My jaw dropped, not sure if I was hearing her right.

"Shouldn't you be resting?" Daisy asked, and Cherisse let out a barked laugh.

"Probably, but my mountain and my elves need me. And Aella is right. We can't defend this portal right now. Not like this. If we bring the mountain down on top of it, we control it on our terms. We can easily tunnel back through to it when we're ready to mount a proper attack. One we've got more time to plan for and know will work."

"At the moment, the dark elf isn't giving us the chance to do anything but react," Sierrathen said. "And worry."

"Exactly," the general added, banging his fist on the table. It shook some of the pieces over, making him look apologetic.

Simon looked at Cherisse and then me, but the cult leader's attention was entirely on me.

"I understand I have you to thank for standing here still," she said as if there were just the two of us in the room.

"You were hurt. And your people need you. I did what any elf with power should do. I made sure you survived to look after them."

"You could easily not have, especially after everything that's happened. You've shown me why you're the Henera and not anyone else. Why this prophecy can come true if we give it a chance. My elves and I will follow you into battle and follow your lead. If you're wading into danger to defend this entire planet, not just my home on it, I'll go with you."

"We'll make sure you and your elves have a place you can call home as soon as possible. And we'll defend that like we do the Sanctuary and warehouse," I replied.

"Then let's stop talking about this and start making it happen. And we'll show this dark elf he can't divide us or make us lose focus on the bigger picture. We'll show him the Henera has everything she needs to beat him."

"Hear, hear," the general cried.

Ronan bowed low, sweeping his torso down as he bent a leg. The others followed suit, Cherisse giving me a small curtsy beside Sierrathen and Daisy. I didn't think Simon was going to join the others, but when the general bowed as well, and he was the only one who hadn't, he exhaled.

"I made you from nothing but DNA samples because I believed in what you would one day be capable of," he said. "I'd be a fool if I stood in your way and didn't offer you my support as well."

I couldn't speak, feeling strange while everyone, even Zephyr, bowed to me. I was a waitress from LA. Or I had been. Yet here I was about to lead an entire army into battle and fling everything I had at the enemy inside a mountain.

"Okay," I said, hoping everyone would rise and stop bowing to me. "Let's move out. We begin the attack in four hours."

It felt strange setting a time on what we were doing, but it broke the moment, and the majority of the leaders in the room scurried off to make sure we had everything we needed and that everyone else who could rest between now and then did so.

"You should sleep as much as possible," Minsheng said as he gave me the helmet back. "Although I'd put whatever magic you think you can spare into these stones. The earth one hasn't gone down much, but the air one is what feels like a quarter of the power, and the water and fire ones are probably about half depleted."

I sighed as I took the helmet back. I'd hoped it would hold more than that, but I knew how much I'd used it in the last battle. It had kept Cherisse alive and made sure the elves at both of the other exits had been kept inside. It was more valuable than anything else I owned and I would likely drain it entirely in the next battle.

"Get the tablets we have spread out and get as many elves as you can to do the same with those," I said instead of voicing my thoughts. It was the best compromise I could make.

"It will be done. Rest and trust us to do our parts." Minsheng gently nudged me toward the tent.

*He has a point. We should rest for a few hours. We're going to have to fight hard, and there's something I want to do before the battle.* Zephyr tugged on my hand, leading me back to the small tent that made up our living quarters.

I was about to ask what that could be when I heard a chuckle from Sen, the small myconid riding Roth while Nuri sat on my shoulder, head tucked beneath his wing.

Pizza. Zephyr wanted to eat pizza before the battle. And I couldn't blame him.

The smell of hot melted cheese and caramelized onion wafted under my nose as Zephyr stirred beside me. I opened my eyes to see several large platters of pizza on the small table in our tent and a grinning Minsheng. Daisy was with him, along with Erlan, Emily, and Newton.

Minsheng grabbed my arm as I held it out and hauled me to my feet.

"We're moving out in about half an hour. We figured we had enough time for this, and the elves in the kitchen were more than happy to oblige when we told them it was part of your traditional battle prep."

"Careful, you'll make it sound as if the Henera makes demands and has these superstitions about fighting and winning."

*If it meant people regularly brought us pizza, would it be bad to let a rumor or two spread?* Zephyr asked, making me grin, but I didn't hesitate to join the others. Pizza for breakfast might have been strange, but Zephyr was right. Pizza was pizza, and I wasn't going to say no.

We didn't think about what was going to happen and instead focused on the food in front of us and the company we had. We talked of adventures we'd had, training sessions that had made Minsheng shake his head in despair or amusement, and of better times when the fate of the world hadn't been on our shoulders.

All too soon the pizza was gone, however, and Minsheng got to his feet.

I lifted the helmet and my small bag, putting them on. I could feel the power in the gemstones, their support invaluable. It wasn't as full as it had been at the start of the previous battle, but I'd done my best to add more, especially to the air stone. When the mountain collapsed, I would need to make sure there was something in there to help me get into the air and away from the worst of the explosion.

*I'll be by your side the whole time*, Zephyr said, still in human form.

I took his hand again and held it in mine.

"Okay," I said, looking at the others. "Let's do this. Let's show the dark elf that we're more badass than he is."

Daisy grinned as she picked up her rifle, and Emily grabbed a strange water cannon device. Newton changed color, going almost black, and Sen and Nuri settled themselves on my shoulders.

As a group, we walked out of the tent and toward the entrance of the main cavern. Many of the others had gathered, groups forming up at designated positions. We were going to do this in several waves, making sure that we used our resources wisely and kept as many of us alive as possible.

All the most powerful elves were going in the first wave armed with tablets, food, and water. With us would be a very select few who couldn't be worked without. People like Minsheng, who were needed to seek out the powerful lieutenant elves we'd encountered once already.

I was going to tackle those one by one and make sure that they weren't a drain on the rest of our elves. And then I had one other goal. The portal and whatever lay between me and it.

It would give the other fighters and elves with me the best chance possible to overcome the rest of the forces and get out before the mountain went down. And if it didn't work, it meant they stood the best chance of running away.

Of course, it wasn't likely to be that simple, but I had to start somewhere and hope.

With Zephyr close by and my party of elves who would keep barriers up and keep us safe alongside me, I strode forward, nodding at Cherisse, Ronan, Sierrathen, the major, and Simon as they each took places commanding other groups and units.

It was a strange sight, seeing so many mythicals, elves, dwarves, centaurs, and humans lined up together, every group but mine having some of each with them. We were truly an alliance of everyone represented on earth. And we were working together.

Feeling my heart swell with pride at the same time as adrenaline coursed through me, I took a deep breath and began my attack. Most familiar with the stairwell, and knowing it was the best single route to clear for everyone following me, I strode toward it.

Several soldiers and elves manned defenses by the small entrance to it and they moved to the side for us as we came closer, the soldiers saluting and the elves lowering their heads briefly.

"Let's send these dark elves back home," I said, not yelling it but hearing others repeat the words like a chant.

Send the dark elves back home.

It rippled outward as I felt into the stairwell with my mind, the air and how it moved, giving away the presence of some air and earth elves inside.

I swept one group aside with an air blast as Zephyr morphed the ground up and around the feet of the second group, fixing them in place.

"Have at them," I said as Sen, Minsheng, and several of the soldiers in the entrance then leaned in. Minsheng threw a light inside to light up the elves for everyone else, and we kept the elves pinned in place while the people with us and Sen filled the elves with feathery darts and took them out.

It was quick and efficient, but I heard a cry from farther up the stairs. It was all the surprise advantage we were going to get. They knew we were attacking them.

I tried not to worry as I reached farther ahead and felt more elves at regular intervals up the stairs and guarding the exits to each floor. We were going to have to take them out along the way and draw the attention of the dark elves on each floor as we did. Thankfully, more of our elves weren't far behind and they'd fan out, sweeping the entire dwelling room by room.

*We've got this*, Zephyr reminded me. *We know this stairwell better than anyone else alive right now.*

Grinning, I took comfort in Zephyr's words. He was right. We'd hidden in them before they'd been brought back into use again, and we'd gone up and down them in the dark. We could do the same one last time.

Still holding hands with him, I blasted the next set of elves from behind, bringing them toward us and toppling one down the stairs.

Roth caught the first one and Minsheng the second and then they were out cold, their limp forms being floated away by another air elf. They could be added to the prisoners we already had.

I tried not to worry about what I might find, knowing the four main elementals were going to be displaying insane amounts of power, and Minsheng would need to find them for me.

"I think I can feel the first one. There's something strange happening in a room about a third of the way up," Minsheng said, his voice barely above a whisper.

As the barrier around me and held in place by an air elf blocked a dart meant for Zephyr or Roth, I exhaled. This wasn't going to be a short battle.

# CHAPTER TWENTY-FIVE

Several more floors up, after fighting past a couple of larger groups of elves and getting back up to thin them down swiftly, we reached the right floor. Here Minsheng thought I'd find at least one of the dark elves with more power and more awareness. One of the dark elves who posed the biggest threat.

I paused, gathering myself for whatever might be ahead. I still had everyone beside me, and so far, we'd not met with any strong resistance that had me worried I couldn't cope. There must be a lot more elves somewhere in the mountain, however. And I was going to be on a floor out of the way for a while. This was the riskiest part of the plan, but it would become easier as I got closer to the top.

With every corner we approached, I grew tenser, expecting to meet with resistance on the other side or elves lying in wait to attack me.

After every corner, I was disappointed, however, until I found myself coming to a door to what looked like a lab at the end of a long corridor. I slowed, noticing that

Minsheng's device was pointing directly to the room ahead. Whatever was in there was causing a huge power spike similar to the feel of the dark elves trying to push through the portal.

I took a few breaths to calm myself down and waited for everyone to catch up with me before I took charge. Turning the handle with one hand, I blasted the door open with air and then strode through.

Rather than finding one of the powerful dark elves, I found a group of more normal elves gathered around a strange device. They backed up, and the machine whirred down.

Before any of them could react, I hit them with another blast of air, pushing them back from the device as I power-ran over to it. Zephyr came with me as Sen started peppering the nearest elves with ice bolts and darts. Minsheng followed as I noticed the device had several large gemstones sitting in the middle of it.

I reached out to them with my mind, feeling the energy they contained. These elves had been powering them up the same way the gemstones in my helmet were charged.

They felt weak and quickly drained, but I wasn't going to test them in the middle of a battle.

*Sen, get the stones and put them in a pocket,* I said.

She jumped down from my shoulder and ran over to grab them. At the same time, the rest of us focused on taking out the elves, hitting them with elements and darts until they were unconscious.

Unlike in previous battles where small pockets of cult elves or soldiers might surrender to us, the dark elves never did so, fighting to the last person and the last bit of power in them if still conscious. It was draining in a whole new way.

As soon as every one of them was neutralized, most of them knocked out with darts, I made my way to Minsheng's side.

"Sorry," he said as soon as he noticed me. "I thought that there must be a powerful elf in here."

"It's okay. If you can get the machine out of here, do so, but we've got the gemstones if not."

"I'll do what I can with it. If not, we'll get Chris in here quickly to look at it and see if he can figure out how it works."

I nodded as Sen tucked the gemstones the elves had been charging into my pocket.

Waiting only long enough for my team to regroup and for Chris and another small unit to arrive to take the machine and any dark elves still living with them, I made my way back to the stairwell.

I felt calmer when I found a group of Amcika and Sanctuary elves, along with the major and his best soldiers, waiting for me to return to the main route.

"It's been quiet so far," the major whispered, his jaw set.

"They know we're coming. At some point, they're going to hit us with everything they've got. You'd best all make sure you're behind me." I exhaled as I finished speaking, realizing that I might have to hold against one massive assault from the dark elves in the mountain while the allies with me got themselves in place to help.

*You won't be alone*, Zephyr said, reminding me.

I squeezed his hand as I threw a barrier around myself and the front line defenders with me. As I'd once seen

Simon do, I drew the air into separate layers, making it colder. I also used the fire abilities I had to draw heat directly out elsewhere, putting the residual heat into a canister Chris had designed.

As I continued, I realized that I'd been using the fire ability longer than I'd thought. The air barrier I kept cold similarly to Simon was done by combining the two elemental abilities, but was that how Simon did it? Did he have enough control over the fire element to harness his air abilities that little bit better?

The Sanctuary had informed me in the past that almost no one had two elements, and if they did, the second was usually considerably weaker. Was Simon an exception?

I had no idea, and I wasn't about to ask him now. Instead, I kept climbing, using the air to help to save my legs some.

We went up another ten floors or so, getting to the levels where most of the elves' communal areas were and past the laboratories. I slowed as we climbed this area, hearing the sound of a small clash and argument on a floor below. Some of the elves and soldiers were responsible for making sure that we cleared the floors as we went past them, and I had as much warning as possible of a potential ambush.

The noise soon subsided and the stairwell went quiet again, nothing coming to my ears but the swish of clothing and the tread of boots as they walked up steps. It was too quiet. Far too quiet.

Sure we were walking into an ambush or trap some-where, I was as quiet and stealthy as I could be. But knowing something was a trap and that I would have to be careful didn't change one very important detail. We had to go on, and I had to fight everything and everyone who got in our way.

A tenseness radiating through my muscles, I wound around the staircase yet again.

In the gloom ahead, I could make out the opening of another floor, the area strangely darker and colder than the previous floors had been. I tried to brighten it and bring more warmth to it, but I met with resistance and the control of others in the air and earth.

Already preparing for battle, I heard the cry of an angry set of elves. At the same time, a large blast of water rushed down the stairs, hitting the barrier with a roar and splitting to either side.

Barely a second later, elves ran out of the nearest floor opening, hurling air blasts at anyone who looked to be out on their own. My barrier held up against that as well, but I soon felt the combined power of so many elves trying to get control of the barrier that I had to motion for the air elves with me to help.

While they were merging their strength and trying to help with the barrier protecting us, the water continued to rush down, spreading out again once it was past me and making it harder for those following behind to move without risking being swept downward.

"Can we get someone like Cherisse and the other water elves to take control of that?" I said aloud to Minsheng. "Preferably without getting rid of it."

Minsheng nodded and pocketed his device, making sure it was on in case it helped him locate the powerful dark elves. He had taken a couple of steps away from me when it beeped and he paused.

I didn't need him to tell me where the powerful elves were, however. I could feel their minds as they took control of so much. They were stronger than any others I'd faced, and they unleashed attack after attack.

*The earth elf is below us as well,* Zephyr said a moment later.

*Below? How did they get below us? We've been clearing the floors out as we go.*

*Could have made another route down. They are earth elves.*

It was a good point, and it made me grit my teeth and clench my fists in fury. Our elves were about to be caught from three sides in a pincer move I hadn't been able to prevent.

They weren't going to give me time to think about regretting it more, however. My mind strained under the pressure to hold as the barrier took the brunt of yet more water and air.

Grateful I couldn't feel the fire elf yet despite his twin being nearby, I hurled air back. At the same time, I wobbled as the entire stairwell shook and several elves fell over.

I used air to catch them as best I could and get them back on their feet.

*Can you get the rock around us and hold it steady?* I asked Zephyr.

*On it already. Working with Sanctuary elves.*

The words were a relief as Cherisse appeared close to me.

"Is that water bitch back?" she asked, her face determined.

"Yup, and she's all yours to fight," I replied, grinning as I realized that left me the air elf.

"Tell me I can help," Simon added as I noticed him and Sierrathen stepping up.

"Hold the barrier. You're better at them than me anyway. I'm going to teach their air elementals a lesson or two."

"I wouldn't miss witnessing that for anything," Cherisse added, her eyes lighting up.

Hoping everyone was up to their tasks, I focused. Letting the air elves with me hold the barrier against the enemy freed up my mind to take some of the air in the stairwell on the other side of the barrier. I reached far beyond the air elves standing near the floor entrance, and I hit them from both sides.

The blast hit them hard enough it banged them into each other and knocked them off their feet, those who could also form barriers bumped by those who wobbled. I fixed my eyes on the air lieutenant in the middle of it all, determined that this one wasn't going to get away.

With the main air elemental in my sights and the rest of the battle ignored, for now, I reached into my pocket until I could feel the gemstones Sen had stashed there. At the same time, as Sen pulled out her little dart gun, Nuri launched into the air, and Roth stepped back to block another wave of water, fueling himself and diverting it into the current floor.

As Nuri turned into a firebolt and I pulled the heat out of the water, we hit them with ice, air, and fire, and I started twirling it around. With help from my mythicals and their abilities, I soon had the ice flying around the dark air elves, Nuri dry in the small barrier I then created around him.

The heat he radiated off grew more intense as I made the funnel smaller.

Several times the air elf tried to challenge me for control of the twister, but drawing on the gemstone in my hand and the one in my helmet was enough to keep them at bay until enough of the air elves around them were flung around and removed from the battle, their bodies blasted into walls, floors, and ceilings until many lay limp somewhere else.

The pressure appeared to ease on Simon and the other air elves, and some of them added their control to mine, Simon's eyes going wide as he felt what I was doing.

"Reckon you can keep it up?" I asked over the din, trying to ignore the guilt at hurting so many elves, enemy or not.

"No idea, but I'd love to try."

"Good. I only need it a minute or so more," I replied.

Taking a deep breath, I let go of everything and focused on the air elf.

*Got those darts ready, Sen?* I asked the dryad on my shoulder while the few remaining air elves were contending with Nuri, Roth, and Simon, as well as the hurricane, water, and fire heading their way.

*Sen ready.*

I heard her cheer as she put the little dart gun to her lips.

*Fly*, I said, seeing her little form wrapped in the tiny suit of dragon scale armor Daisy had made her, the little flying prototype on her back from Chris, and her bright little eyes one of the only parts of her not protected.

She jetted off my shoulder, and I helped her along. With the distractions and the fire, water, and twister to keep her obscured, the air elf didn't see her coming. I helped her take aim, stilling the air in a funnel as Simon's control on the twister finally lapsed, and it died enough.

The darts hit the elf in rapid succession, Sen's practice and my abilities making sure she never missed.

It took four darts, the sedatives combating the adrenaline and whatever the air elf did to combat it until the air elf slumped to the floor.

The floor went quiet and I heard the air elves with me cheer, but we weren't done yet. Roth blocked another blast of water, sliding back down several steps as he did. The force was too strong for him to do anything but absorb and diffuse until I lent my mind to Cherisse and took the edge off the stream, hitting the control of whoever had sent it.

As soon as Roth recovered, he ran backward, down the stairwell and to Zephyr's side. I grinned as Nuri went that way as well and Sen flew back to me.

This time I took control of the water gemstone in my pocket and I began moving the water out of the way, my reach going up and around the water elves. They'd diverted the river that fed the mountain and everyone in it, running it in a spiral funnel down the center of the stairwell for a while. It was a clever idea, but it was going to backfire on them.

I moved closer, getting Simon to bring the barrier with me as I focused. Finding the place they had diverted the water, I took control of the earth and quickly started to shift it back on the old path.

In almost no time, the water stopped flowing, and the water elves had nothing to work with but what had remained. I saw the twin growl and try to step back, but I quickly threw a barrier up behind her.

She let out a defiant roar, her anger coming off her in waves that made the water in the air stand still before rushing toward me. As Cherisse took another couple of steps forward, however, more water elves with their leader, the liquid dropped harmlessly to the floor, and I had a clear path.

Minsheng shot with his rifle several times, having been choosing his targets carefully and holding his own in a group of elementals.

I helped those darts hit, satisfied when he also took out another of the dark water elves. Sen got another set of elves in quick succession as they pulled back.

Within another couple of minutes, the water elves were dealt with as well, and the path before us was clear. I exhaled, feeling some of the elves with me relax.

"Keep the barrier up and hold here," I said, turning to head back to Zephyr. No sooner had I done so than I felt him, Nuri, and Roth returning up the stairs, the ground beneath my feet under Zephyr's control.

*Earth elemental dealt with*, Zephyr informed me.

I grinned as he joined us, my mythicals with me again. Then we focused on heading up once more. There was still a fire elf to contend with and whatever forces were hiding near the portal, but we were making progress, and they were getting weaker.

# CHAPTER TWENTY-SIX

We bypassed more floors, meeting resistance when a group of dark elves appeared to be guarding one of the main floors of sleeping rooms. I suspected they were a group we had woken, their abilities waning fast as if they'd begun the fight drained.

The sedated or otherwise incapacitated elves were taken back down the mountain, and I pushed on, hoping that the elves and soldiers behind me were doing their job. They were supposed to be laying strategically placed charges, some made from traditional sources and explosives. A few of them were being charged by me as I went, devices that stored phenomenal amounts of elemental power.

I tried to give the soldiers everything they needed, but I was aware there was still the fire elf. I would have plenty of heat to funnel then.

After passing the main living floor, I noticed a slight difference in the feel of the elements. They had felt marked in the past and in a lot of ways that was no different, but there was something different about them now. They felt slimy and slippery. I'd felt something similar in one other place, on the other side of the portal.

My mind fixed on memories of reaching my control through and how several times the dark elf had connected to me. It had felt similar then, and it might be a bad sign that he was nearby or in the building.

So far there was no sign of him, and if he was here, I could feel the marker he left behind, not his power. It comforted me that Minsheng hadn't detected him either, the device he was using only faintly detecting more elves ahead.

As I went around one of the last bends before we reached the portal floor, the air was growing hotter and staler as if it was held in place.

I grabbed one of the strange storage devices that could become a powerful charged explosive and began sucking the heat back out again. Zephyr did the same, making it clear we were preparing for something.

"Get the fire elves up here," Cherisse said, not waiting for me to make the same request.

I nodded my gratitude at her as Simon got the other air elves to work with him to keep the air barrier in place.

"Can you keep the barrier cold?" I asked.

"If a fire elf helps me," he replied.

"Count me in," Erlan added as Newton ran down his arm and along to Roth. The two creatures had become firm friends when they realized the fire salamander could heat his water streams.

Zephyr and I strode forward together, channeling heat

and not letting anyone else follow us until we deemed it safe.

There was still no sign of the fire elf, but I drew on the fire gemstone anyway, knowing it was one of the least depleted elements in the helmet I wore. I tried not to worry as we still didn't find him or the other fire elves who must be in the mountain somewhere.

I reached out as far as I could with the air, noticing the temperatures grew hotter as it went up, even beyond the portal room.

*Block off the stairs above the portal floor,* Zephyr suggested. *We can do it together.*

*You think they're up there.*

*It's where I'd be with fire elves. And something molten and hot that could flow downstairs. We'd need to block it as it melted everything. It would wreck the stairs so fast it would strand everyone on different floors, divide us, and stop us from going back down.*

*We'll need to divert it if you're right,* I replied. Fear made my stomach turn.

"Get us some earth elves," Zephyr said barely above a whisper.

The message echoed back as we held our ground.

"And everyone, prepare to run for the portal floor," I added, hoping we wouldn't get stuck on that floor with no way to leave it other than the portal.

Our words and the serious tone soon had everyone around us taking the possible threat seriously. We didn't have time to explain the danger to them, but I was sure Zephyr was right as I pushed my mind to its limits and felt the fire elf, off to one side in a doorway to a floor several levels above the portal.

He was on his knees, other elves around him, their hands reaching out for each other.

Not wanting to disturb them and break their concentration in case they let go of whatever they were holding onto, I simply joined Zephyr and the earth elves who were following his lead and grew a wall, making it thicker between the portal and them.

It wasn't easy, especially as the air continued to grow hotter and more uncomfortable while we were otherwise focused. The wall we were creating heated as we were building it. Whatever the fire elves were doing, they were putting us in trouble.

"Fire elves. We need our fire elves," I said, not sure where they'd gotten to.

"They're almost here," Cherisse replied as she closed her eyes. "Can you make a funnel for some water through that wall of yours? I can cool it down and create a heat sink with some water."

I lifted my eyebrows in surprise, but I loved the idea. I reached with my mind toward the river again. Using a similar idea to the elves in the lower part of the mountain, I created a route for the river to loop through, running through the wall Zephyr was creating and then threading the water back and forth as Cherisse advised.

It was perfect teamwork, and Zephyr, the rest of the earth elves, and I started making the wall thicker and more stable as everyone started moving forward again. Our fire elves worked with Erlan, Cherisse, and the water flow to make the wall colder, the water almost freezing before they stopped.

I reached through to the other side of the wall, feeling the position of the dark elves with my mind. They were beginning to back up and it made me think. I grabbed Zephyr's hand and ran up several steps. I could feel everyone coming with me, but I was so focused on trying to stop the dark elves from escaping that I didn't tell them to stop or slow. There was a good chance we needed to move fast anyway.

I reached as deep as I could for the air behind the fire elves, feeling Zephyr respond and push through with me. I grabbed as much of the air as I could, once again drawing on the power of the helmet, the air gemstones we'd found in the lab drained. This time I threw it hard and fast.

We caught the fire elves in the back, sending them sprawling forward. Nervous as they scrambled away again and the air heated more. I reached in the opposite direction to their hurried scramble while trying to keep the air blasts up to make it hard for them to get away.

It didn't take long to get an idea of what was happening. As Zephyr had suspected, the fire elves had created a stream of red hot magma, and it had been unleashed.

The burning liquid flowed faster than I'd have thought possible, coming down toward the wall.

"Hurry, everyone," I called. "Out of the stairwell and up to the highest floor you can manage."

Behind me, elves and soldiers rushed upward as we carried on toward the portal floor. The hot magma hit the wall we'd created and steam rose. The dark elves had managed to get back to their feet and were trying to pull away, but I hit them once more, determined to keep them from getting away from the danger until we were.

The steam created in the upper portion of the stairwell made me wonder if I'd made the right choice. The dark elves writhed in the boiling steam, burning and crying out before collapsing.

My stomach churned, and I slowed. When I'd created the wall of water, I had expected the fire elves to be pushed to simply undo what they had created to save their lives. It hadn't occurred to me that they might not have the power left to save themselves.

I gulped as Zephyr dragged me onward. By the time we reached the portal floor, I could see the wall we'd built above. It was beginning to glow and sag.

"Quickly," I called back, stopping to usher everyone past me.

*We need to keep everyone safe from whatever is ahead,* Zephyr said, stopping with me.

*And we also need a route back out, or we won't be able to blow the mountain and not take us with it.*

Zephyr hesitated, his fingers still entwined in mine.

*Do the bare minimum you need to keep a path down open.*

I nodded as I let go of Zephyr, and he hurried to the front of the group of mythicals. Sen stayed on my shoulder, nuzzling into my neck while I used more air to boost the speed of everyone still rushing upward, the soldiers bringing up the rear and carrying more charges between them.

At the same time, I pulled up more cold rock and took more heat out of the wall to keep it standing as long as possible.

By the time the last soldier was coming up toward me, I was sweating and panting, so much heat in the area that my abilities were doing very little to change it. The wall gave way despite my best efforts, and I had to take a step back.

Not sure I could do much more until the heat came out of the molten rock on its own, no longer fueled by anything, I backed up and then powered myself toward Zephyr and the others.

The tug in my stomach lessened as I ran toward them and the portal room.

It didn't take long for me to hear the sounds of commotion, yelling, and battle ahead. It spurred me on to run faster, the air I controlled pushing my limbs to a greater speed.

The elves ahead moved out of my way, thankfully aware that I was going to want to get back to the front of our battle line. I soon found Zephyr standing beside Simon, the pair holding the air barrier in front. Cherisse was farther back with Roth and Sierrathen. Nuri was flying overhead, and I admired his seemingly boundless energy for a second before rushing back to Zephyr's side.

We were still a long way from the part of the floor with the portal, but it was clear that the last line of elves was protecting this floor, so many of them ahead and packed in that I gulped.

For a second I wasn't sure if we were going to get any farther, knowing that these were fresh fighters and everyone with me had been in battles and drained their abilities in several ways.

But the dark elves ahead of me didn't have any extra

supplies, soldiers with tranquilizer guns, nor, it seemed, the tech that we possessed. It might still give us the advantage we needed, and I had to believe and hope that it would.

I set my jaw and reached out with my mind once more. It was time to give these elves something to fight against and push through to the portal. I needed to hold the cavern it sat in for long enough that the soldiers could place the last of the charges. And I needed to make sure the main dark elf didn't appear from the planet on the other side.

With Erlan, Cherisse, and Zephyr closest to me and Simon holding the barrier, we had one good team to push this group of dark elves back.

"One element each," I said quietly, more for Zephyr's benefit than anyone else's. "Let's clear out this mountain."

I gritted my teeth, snatched control of as much of the air as I could, and hit the dark elves closest with it before they could respond. I was satisfied to see several go over and bump into others, distracting some of the earth elves long enough that Zephyr grabbed more control.

With a quick maneuver he was well-practiced in, the ground moved like it was anything but solid rock and grabbed feet and other limbs, pinning the elves in place.

The soldiers took advantage of it, and Cherisse found a water source to spray a group of dark elves off their feet. Nuri darted forward like a bolt, zapping fire from his mouth and becoming a large ball of fire at the same time.

I walked forward despite the dark elves not falling back and encouraged Simon and the air elves acting as his support to come with me.

The dark elves responded, challenging me for control,

but I didn't let up. I used the helmet to boost me and push back. There was a wider section a few hundred yards away, where we would have a wider front, where we would be able to bring some of the soldiers forward and have them shoot past us more easily.

While the elves would run out of power eventually, the soldiers had enough ammo and guns that we could keep shooting until the mountain was clear and then some.

It was the backup we truly needed in a situation like this. But the humans were also the most vulnerable of us and the most easily hurt. I needed to make sure we didn't forget to protect them in the chaos.

The dark elves acted in teams, someone yelling instructions I didn't understand from near the back. It brought them into units, some of them defending, some of them challenging us for control, and others hitting us with the elements similarly to us hitting them.

After a while of not making enough progress, I looked for Minsheng and signaled for him to begin passing out the stone tablet fragments we had. Zephyr reached for the dagger he had strapped to himself, his human form wearing it around his neck, while in dragon form, it was attached to one of the large central horns on the back of his head.

Able to control the earth element even better, the dagger hilt contained a small pile of seeds. Zephyr scattered some of these now, growing plants that he quickly used to restrain dark elves.

With the tablets helping to power some of the more skilled elves, we pushed forward again. My helmet was almost entirely drained, but it was no longer needed for anything but the air element to help us fly out when we were done.

In the meantime, I switched up what elements I was using, trying to be more unpredictable. I hit the elves with water and then took control of the plants to hit them with the growing vines. Following that with a fireball or two, I took out several more dark elves.

Finally, we pushed them back to an area where we could spread out and bring more soldiers up to help us beat back the dark elves.

Pausing to take a rifle from a soldier, I missed a couple of fire elves taking aim at me. Thankfully my phoenix noticed and dived to take the hit, the fire adding to his own.

I exhaled, promising myself to be more careful and aware. Keeping myself alive was just as important as the soldiers around me.

Forming one part of an impressive line of fighters, I lifted the rifle and looked for some easier targets, taking shots and using my abilities.

We were making progress and so far we were surviving, but there had been a lot of elves inside the mountain, more than we'd feared. We weren't done yet and we were getting tired.

# CHAPTER TWENTY-SEVEN

With an ache forming in my head, I stopped and grabbed some more ammo for the rifle I carried. There was a pile of dark elves now, the bodies mostly sporting feathered darts, but some had been taken out of the fight in other ways.

I tried not to worry about dark elf deaths and instead focused on what I could control, the vines Zephyr was working with being shared between us as we pulled dark elves off their feet and suspended them upside down and out of the way.

Once a soldier managed to shoot over the crowds and knock the temporarily restrained soldiers out, we put the sedated dark elves down, although we weren't being gentle. I dropped another, and Zephyr threw out a scatter of seeds closer to the dark elves to help cause more chaos.

Finally, the dark elves broke and fell back, giving us the ground to push forward and into the portal cavern. I could finally see the large opening to another dimension, but none of the elves seemed to want to go through it.

Despite their reluctance, I started blasting them with air towards it, working with other air elves to herd them.

It didn't entirely work. A dark elf, who wore robes that distinguished his difference from the others, called the elves back. Given the position he was in, he didn't appear to be as concerned as I'd have expected.

Frowning, I pushed forward, wanting to get this battle over and done with. What did he know that we didn't?

The elves gave way until I was standing not far from the portal, the dark elves ignoring me to hit the elves behind me. I felt the sensation of another mind reaching out to connect to the elements within my control. And it was a grip I recognized.

*Careful, Aella,* Zephyr said. *This is beginning to feel like another trap.*

I didn't disagree but I needed to buy time for the soldiers to get the last of the charges in place.

*Get as many dark elves dealt with as you can and I'll distract the dark elf, if nothing else,* I replied as I focused. The connection was rough, and I could feel him attempting to penetrate my defenses and the same slimy reach as he tried to move along my bonds.

Nuri landed on my shoulder, the phoenix experienced in helping rebuff the control of the evil elf. I appreciated the advice and support as Sen got down and scurried off.

*Dark elf feeds off fear. Calm, Aella, and concentrate.*

Nuri continued to whisper words of encouragement as I pushed and held back, focusing on holding against the attack. I drew on the helmet, making sure the air gemstone was still left untouched, but the dark elf pushed harder than I'd ever felt before.

*Oh, Henera*, his voice suddenly broke, echoing around my mind and bringing a throbbing headache with it.

I didn't reply, trying to push him out and keep him out. Nuri didn't give up either, the strength of the phoenix's bond with me clear as I realized it felt less slimy and the pain was bothering Nuri less.

Making a mental note to get Nuri to teach Roth, Sen, and Zephyr how to fight the dark elf more themselves as well, I took a few steps back, each one making my head swim.

If it had been harder for me to reach deeper and my abilities grew weaker with each yard my mind was through a portal and beyond myself, then I was sure the same was true for the dark elf. Any advantage I could get, I was going to take.

*You're stronger than I expected for someone so divided*, the voice continued. *I'm sure you give everyone hope. But you're so fragile, and you still have so much to learn.*

*Everyone is always learning.* My voice seemed strange as I talked back. It earned me a condescending chuckle.

*Is that what gives you hope? The ridiculous notion that you could learn something I don't know and use it against me? Oh, my sweet young elf. You have some hard lessons to learn.*

*And you have some arrogance to unlearn*, I replied, pushing back hard in the way Nuri was suggesting. My mind quickly resisted him, shutting him out of my head again.

I closed my eyes and focused on the disgusting feeling being connected with him gave me. Bit by bit, I unraveled the connection and took another couple of steps back.

Although I couldn't be sure, it felt as if the dark elf let go a little as well, the pressure no longer as bad.

"I don't think I can buy much more time," I said aloud, hoping that whoever needed to hear me would.

"We only need another minute or so," the major replied from somewhere to my left.

I nodded and this time, I reached to keep hold of the dark elf. Deciding to explore the connection the other way and see what I could learn about him, I pushed along the connection in reverse, latching on.

*Careful. It is not a good thing to force,* Nuri said. *It is not how our magic is supposed to be used.*

Nuri's words made me more cautious, but I wasn't sure how else to keep the dark elf occupied for longer. His control could cause havoc in other ways and I didn't want to be fighting him as he attacked the others.

Although I sensed disapproval from Nuri, he continued to help me until the major came before us.

"Done. Time to go, Aella."

No sooner had the major finished speaking than some dark elves blasted him with air. I caught him and stopped him from getting hurt. It forced me to let go of the connection with the dark elf and pull back.

"Get everyone out. I'll hold the line," I said, aware there were still a lot of dark elves to fight.

If the example the dark elves had set in battle so far was anything to go by, then they were going to fight until the end.

Zephyr came to my side as Sen bounded onto my shoulder and Roth galloped closer.

*Cherisse is going to get everyone out. They've asked for ten minutes, and then we need to get out as well,* Zephyr explained.

*Can they get back down the stairs?*

*Some earth elves were working on making a route through now that the magma has cooled.*

I exhaled in relief. Somehow we'd managed to make this work, but I was beginning to feel drained, and there were a lot of dark elves still standing.

I stood there with my mythicals, the dark elves coming forward as I looked them over. No one attacked, but they came around me. I thought they were going to block us off.

"I don't know any of you. Your names. What kind of life you've led. Or why you're here. But I don't want to fight you if I don't have to. I don't want anything but to defend my home from the dark elf who would destroy it or use and abuse it."

This made them pause, some of them glancing at each other. It made me wonder if anyone had talked to them before now.

"Can you come with me? Will you come with me? Leave here and stop this? There's an elven Sanctuary on this planet. And I have a large home. We'd find somewhere for you. Somewhere you don't have to fight. Somewhere you could live freely and happily."

As I spoke, Zephyr turned into his dragon form. Many of the dark elves stepped back, and I couldn't help but grin.

"We don't know if we can trust you," their lieutenant replied, stepping forward. "You are the slayer. The elf created to destroy us all."

"Not according to the prophecy I'm supposed to be fulfilling. I'm supposed to be the elf saving everyone."

"This is what Kirdash tells us of himself. How do we know which one of you speaks the truth? You attack us, and he feeds and clothes us. You drain us, and he trains us."

I nodded, understanding that my words were going to do nothing to persuade them.

*Sen help*, the dryad said from my shoulder, jumping down. She put her dart gun down and bounded up to one of the plants Zephyr's vine weapon had created. *Aella, make it fruit.*

Willing to give the dark elves a change and follow Sen's advice, I grew the vine taller and produced fruit. Roth stepped closer, tossing his head several times and watering the plant for me. Flowers grew, quickly pollinated by Sen, and then they fruited.

At the same time, Zephyr flew up and launched himself at the cavern ceiling. It had been repaired since we'd broken the pillars and Zephyr had flown me out that way, but his main role in the last twenty minutes had been to make it weaker.

He broke a chunk through, grabbing the rock before it could fall, but letting the sunlight in. Within seconds I could use the environment we'd created to make the fruit grow and ripen.

As soon as it was ready, Sen leaped into the air and grabbed one. She then ran it over to the dark elf in charge, no hint of fear in her body.

I watched, barely daring to breathe as the elf took it and brought it up to his face. I feared that the elf wouldn't take the chance on it, suspecting a trap, but I looked as unconcerned as possible and gave the elf time. If nothing else this was buying my allies time to get out of the mountain.

Zephyr landed beside me again, coming in close as Sen retreated and bounded onto Roth's back. This was the moment it would turn one way or another.

The elf finally took a bite, everyone watching him as he chewed slowly and then took another one.

I raised my eyebrows, having expected one mouthful either way. After a second, the dark elf lowered the fruit and looked at me.

"It seems there is at least some truth to your words. You're capable of care. But it is not enough to show us that this is possible and yet ask us to trust you. Our leader promises us this is already possible here. We can do this without you."

There was nothing more I could do, and I knew it.

"You should go back through the portal before it is too late," I said, sure the ten minutes was up. "This mountain is coming down. There is nothing any of you can do to stop it. Any of you who wish to trust me are welcome to fly up and out with me, but I leave the rest of you to either flee through the portal or perish. Your choice."

I gave everyone a moment longer before I used the air gemstone to give myself one final burst of power to get onto Zephyr's back. Nuri and Roth quickly followed, the latter carrying Sen.

Although I still had a little of my power left, I might need it if I was followed by a lot of the dark elves, but very few of them came.

I kept looking down, checking if any were going to follow. Some of the dark elves did take one of the suggestions, diving back through the portal as Zephyr took us higher.

Panting and exhausted, I lay against the dragon's back, focusing on holding on and helping Roth and Nuri keep with us and clear.

A few of the attackers moved away from the portal, the lieutenant going with them, barking orders, but it was the last thing I saw before Zephyr wheeled away.

*We can do no more to save them*, Zephyr said to me, and I knew he was right.

Zephyr flew toward the safe zone where we could see our allies had gathered. He let out a loud roar, the previously decided signal that we and everyone who had been with us were either clear of the mountain or unable to be saved.

We flew toward the safe area as explosion after explosion sounded behind us, starting with the portal cavern to drop it down within the mountain and then the outsides to collapse it in on top.

Zephyr circled as a small air blast hit us and the mountain rumbled, tumbling. I used the last of the strength I had to wrap us in an air barrier and help protect us from dust and debris that was kicked up even this high until everything settled.

Slowly, we circled toward our friends, their familiar faces filling me with relief. It appeared as if everyone had gotten out safely and they moved toward the rubble of a mountain.

I felt sorry for the cult elves who were looking at their destroyed home. If there had been another way, I'd have chosen it.

As I landed, Cherisse was standing, her eyes on the large pile of rock, her eyes glistening.

"I know there's not a lot I can say to take the pain you're feeling away," I said. "But I hope we can find you somewhere you feel is home again soon. And I hope we can defend it far better in the future."

"It was my stubbornness that resulted in this," Cherisse replied. "I thought I knew best. I clearly didn't. But you're right. We'll find a new home, and we'll rebuild. And we'll make sure the dark elf never gets his hands on this planet."

"Together," I said, giving the water elemental a nod.

It was all that needed to be said. Minsheng handed me a snack and ushered me and my mythicals to a tent where we could rest.

A small team of earth elves would go to make sure the portal was encased in rock and become part of a watch who would keep it that way no matter what the dark elf did. It wasn't a permanent solution, but for now, it would buy us time until I could work out how to close it again and put new pillars into place.

"Rest," Minsheng said. "You've done what you needed to. We're safe, and we've gained a reprieve and knowledge."

Taking the helmet off, I handed it to him, knowing he was one of the few people I would trust to keep it safe.

"The President sends his congratulations on a mission well completed."

I let out a laugh, not sure how I'd gotten to the point that resulted in the President leaving me personal messages. It was something I would contemplate another time, however.

For now, my world was safe once more. It was enough.

## EPILOGUE

Seeing the President face to face was always something I found surreal, but he'd insisted on being there as I went to visit the Texas portal again.

It was almost a week since we'd buried the Mexican portal, and it was still being monitored by a combination of Amcika and Sanctuary elves. There had been no activity.

Most interestingly, and the reason I was here, was that the Texas portal had also been entirely silent and still. At least, until this morning.

"Thank you for coming, Aella, Zephyr, Sen, Roth, Nuri, and Minsheng. Your presence and expertise are always a comfort. I've had lunch laid out, and the portal is being monitored. Currently, it's still once more, but we're hoping that after some food, it won't be again."

I grinned, grateful for the mention of lunch. The President knew the way to get me to like him, and he was respectful of my mythicals as well.

We didn't take long to demolish the grilled chickens and other meats and salads he'd had laid out for us. Then we waited, talking over the security for the site and the Sanctuary and warehouse elves who supplemented the soldiers who guarded it.

Now that the Amcika elves weren't trying to open a portal and it was mostly dormant, there wasn't much for the elves to do and we agreed to reduce the number and let them rest more.

We were trying to work out who could head home when someone came running into the room.

"It's happening, sir," they said as they gave the President a salute.

"Good man," the President replied as he got to his feet.

I did the same and was grateful to be motioned forward. Curiosity had the better of me as I noticed everyone else remained relaxed. Whatever this was about it wasn't a major threat.

As I walked into the portal room, I noticed that the barriers were there again but set back farther than before and appearing to be more robust.

I walked up to them, my mind reaching forward. Minsheng pulled out one of his devices and read the environment.

"Looks like someone is there. Or trying to push through. Not him though."

Unlike the Mexican portal, this one had always felt slightly open, as if it was barely contained. The dark elf had connected to me through it more than once.

Today as I reached forward and toward it, however, I found the connection and reach of a very different elf.

As we connected I felt a very gentle approach, none of

the force or slimy feeling of the dark elf. I let them in, Nuri landing on my shoulder as I did.

*Hello*, I thought, wondering if they could hear me.

*Oh goodness. You're truly there and real. An elf. We hoped what the drones were saying was true.*

*Drones?*

*His workers. Some of them have been through a portal. Did they find you?*

*They may have done. I sent a lot back.*

I heard an almost delighted giggle at this.

*Who are you?* I asked a moment later.

*Another elf, like you. Not everyone here serves the dark elf. Some of us hide or resist. I am a bondslave.*

*That doesn't sound like a good thing.*

*It keeps me alive and fed.*

I had no idea how to respond to her words, so many questions getting half stuck in my mind as I absorbed everything she'd said.

*Are you the Henera? Are you the hope everyone is talking of?*

*Everyone here believes I am the Henera*, I replied.

*All four elements obey you?*

*All four.*

*Yet you haven't opened the portals to rescue us?*

*Until now I had no idea that there was anyone in need of rescue. But if this is true, rest assured, there are many powerful elves here, not just myself. We will-*

*I must go*, she said, interrupting me. *Please, rescue us, Henera. We need you.*

Before I could give any more reassurance the connection vanished and the blocked-off portal went silent and still once more. I kept reaching toward it, holding on to the connection with it and the elements inside the portal area but the woman never returned.

"What happened?" Minsheng asked a moment later.

"I found out what I need to do next," I replied, beginning to process.

*Another mission?* Zephyr said. *Good. After a few days off from saving people from impending doom, I was starting to get bored.*

I started laughing at the sarcasm in Zephyr's voice, knowing that as much as he was making a point that we would do whatever we could. There were elves in danger, and once again we would have to figure out how to rescue them.

The story continues with *Light Sworn*, book 11 in the Dragon of Shadow and Air series.

Claim your copy today!

## ACKNOWLEDGMENTS

Once again I find myself thankful for so many things. It is easy to be so thankful when I am so blessed. Firstly with the most wonderful publisher and people who work there. I could name people, but then I know I would leave others out. They all do their part of the process and make me feel honoured to be one of their authors. And they go above and beyond caring about my books. They also care about me and my well being. The things that matter to me.

To all my readers. You have made these series a dream to write knowing that so many of you are eager to find out what happens next. I've discovered it a little before you but I hope you enjoy this book as much as I did to write even with the ending.

And to Bryan. You have kept me going lately when I wanted to give up. I've known you for so many years and yet I still feel as if there's so much to discover and so many stories to hear. You've given me back some of my confidence and believed in me from the beginning even with the distance between us. I hope I can return the support over the years to come.

To my two tiny humans, who have taught me so much and given me so many emotions and so much to feel. You give me something to fight for, something to rise for and something to stand for.

Finally, to God, who is there in the failure as much as the success.

# ABOUT THE AUTHOR

Jess was born in the quaint village of Woodbridge in the UK, has spent some of her childhood in the States and now resides near the beautiful Roman city of Bath. She lives with her husband, Phil, her two tiny humans (one boy and one girl) and her very dapsy cat, Pleaides.

During her still relatively short life Jess has displayed an innate curiosity for learning new things and has therefore studied many subjects, from maths and the sciences, to history and drama. Jess now works full time as a writer and mummy, incorporating many of the subjects she has an interest in within her plots and characters.

When she's not busy with work and keeping her tiny humans alive she can often be found with friends, playing with miniature characters, dice and pieces of paper covered in funny stats and notes about fictional adventures her figures have been on.

You can find out more about the author and her upcoming projects by joining her on facebook, by watching her live D&D streams, or emailing her via books@jessmountifield.co.uk. Jess loves hearing from a happy fan so please do get in touch!

Jess is also opening up her discord for fans to come chat about what she's up to, and see a few sneak peaks of future work. There's also a chance to become one of her beta readers. If you'd like to check that out you can do so here.

**Connect with Jess Mountifield**

Mailing list sign up
Facebook group.
Discord group
Actual play D&D stream: Twitch or Youtube
Email address: contact me here.

**Already published**

**Urban Fantasy**

**Dragon of Shadow and Air:**

Air Bound

Shadow Sworn

Dragon Souled

Earth Bound

Night Sworn

Dryad Souled

Water Bound

Day Sworn

Pegasus Souled

Fire Bound

**Fantasy**

**Tales of Ethanar:**

Wandering to Belong (Tale 1)

Innocent Hearts (Tale 2 & 3)

For Such a Time as This (Tale 4)

A Fire's Sacrifice (Tale 5)

**Winter Series:**

The Hope of Winter (Tale 6.05)

The Fire of Winter (Tale 6.1)

**Guild of the Eternal Flame:**

Wayfarer's Sanctuary

Protector's Secret

Healer's Oath

**Other Fantasy:**

The Initiate (under Holly Lujah)

**Writing with Dawn Chapman:**

Jessica's Challenge (#5 in the Puatera Online series)

Dahlia's Shadow (#6 in the Puatera Online series)

Lila's Revenge (#7 in the Puatera Online series)

**Sci-Fi:**

**Fringe Colonies:**

Alliance

Haven

Rebellion

Rebirth

Reclamation

**Star Trail:**

Hunted

**Sherdan series:**

Sherdan's Prophecy

Sherdan's Legacy

Sherdan's Country

Sherdan's Road (A short story in the anthology 'The End of the Road')

The Slave Who'd Never Been Kissed (A short in the charity anthology 'Imaginings')

New Beginnings

Santa's Little Space Pirate

**In the multi-author Adamanta series:**

Episode 1 – Adamanta

Episode 3 – Excelsior

Episode 8 – Phoenix

Episode 13 – New Contacts

Episode 17 – Sacrifice

**Other:**

Clues, Claws and Christmas

**Non-Fic:**

How to Write Lots, and Get Sh*t Done: the Art of Not Being a Flake

Find purchase links here

**Coming soon:**

**Urban Fantasy:**

**Dragon of Shadow and Air:**

Light Sworn

Phoenix Souled

**Fantasy**

**(Tales of Ethanar):**

The Pursuit of Winter (#2 in the Winter series, Tale 6.2)

**Books under Amelia Price**

**Mycroft Holmes Adventures:**

The Hundred Year Wait

The Unexpected Coincidence

The Invisible Amateur

The Female Charm

The Reluctant Knight

The Ambitious Orphan

The Unconventional Honeymoon Gift

The Family Reunion

The Immortal Problem

**Coming soon:**

The Unremarkable Assistant